AF098746

SASSY
VIRGIN BRIDE
SONJA

SASSY SONJA
VIRGIN BRIDE

SARAH SEWELL WOLTERS

ReadersMagnet, LLC

Sassy Sonja: Virgin Bride
Copyright © 2022 by *Sarah Sewell Wolters*

Published in the United States of America

ISBN Paperback: 978-1-958030-90-5
ISBN eBook: 978-1-958030-91-2

All rights reserved. No part of this publication may be reproduced, stored in a retrieval system or transmitted in any way by any means, electronic, mechanical, photocopy, recording or otherwise without the prior permission of the author except as provided by USA copyright law.

The opinions expressed by the author are not necessarily those of ReadersMagnet, LLC.

ReadersMagnet, LLC
10620 Treena Street, Suite 380 | San Diego, California, 92131 USA
1.619. 354. 2643 | www.readersmagnet.com

Book design copyright © 2022 by ReadersMagnet, LLC. All rights reserved.

Cover design by Ericka Obando
Interior design by Dorothy Lee

TABLE OF CONTENTS

Chapter One 7
Chapter Two... 13
Chapter Three 18
Chapter Four 24
Chapter Five 29
Chapter Six.. 33
Chapter Seven 38
Chapter Eight 42
Chapter Nine... 46
Chapter Ten... 51
Chapter Eleven... 56
Chapter Twelve.. 60
Chapter Thirteen 64
Chapter Fourteen 68
Chapter Fifteen 72
Chapter Sixteen.. 77
Chapter Seventeen 82
Chapter Eighteen 87
Chapter Nineteen 91
Chapter Twenty.. 94
Chapter Twenty One.. 99
Chapter Twenty Two 103
Chapter Twenty Three 107
Chapter Twenty Four 112
Chapter Twenty Five 116
Chapter Twenty Six... 119
Chapter Twenty Seven 123
Chapter Twenty Eight... 127
Chapter Twenty Nine 131
Chapter Thirty.. 135

Chapter Thirty One	139
Chapter Thirty Two	144
Chapter Thirty Three	149
Chapter Thirty Four	153
Chapter Thirty Five	157
Chapter Thirty Six	160
Chapter Thirty Seven	164
Chapter Thirty Eight	167
Chapter Thirty Nine	171
Chapter Forty	177
Chapter Forty One	181
Chapter Forty Two	184
Chapter Forty Three	187
Chapter Forty Four	191
Chapter Forty Five	194
Chapter Forty Six	197
Chapter Forty Seven	201
Chapter Forty Eight	204
Chapter Forty Nine	208
Chapter Fifty	211
Chapter Fifty One	215
Chapter Fifty Two	220
Chapter Fifty Three	224
Chapter Fifty Four	227
Chapter Fifty Five	231
Chapter Fifty Six	236
Chapter Fifty Seven	240
Chapter Fifty Eight	245

CHAPTER ONE

AUGUST 1955

I really love this room. It is quiet in this little den – hot, but quiet. I need to think this morning. Suddenly my comfortable life is pretty much ruined.

Last night my father announced that we are moving to Jacksonville. We have to move because his lumber business is going "bankrupt". I'm still not quite sure what that means exactly, but I do know that the business he has poured his every waking minute into will not be operating anymore. He was in the Navy in Jacksonville during WWII and wants to go back there where he still has friends who haven't been part of the lumber business. Mom has applied for a job with the Navy.

My father, Jerry Kent, doesn't believe in explaining things to children. He believes in obedience; particularly from me, his only daughter. He hates it when I ask him to spell out anything, it's like I am blaspheming or something if I ask a simple question.

Regardless, last night at dinner I asked.

"What about me?" I had to know. "I need to finish school." Father knew all about my scholarship to Converse College. My piano teacher was an alumni of Converse College and had one nomination for entrance each year. The nomination was mine as soon as I finished the auditions and eligibility requirements. "I have to live here, in Augusta, not down south in Jacksonville."

"Tough," he told me curtly. "Deal with it. You are needed with us in Florida."

While he will tolerate a question under extreme circumstances, like this one, there is absolutely no arguing with my father. Not unless you want a whipping and even if you take it that far, you'd be getting the whipping for nothing because he would never change his mind. I'm only sixteen, not old enough yet to be out on my own. I have no options. Shut up and move, that's my only choice.

It's maddening. It's not fair. What did I do wrong? Nothing. I studied hard, worked harder. My piano teacher, Miss Bloom, says that I could be a professional musician someday, that I have real talent. But what good is talent without instruction? I need to go to college! I didn't "bankrupt" father's business, he did or someone else did, I don't know. It is not fair that my piano will be sold to help pay Dad's debts.

When I called Aunt Mabel this afternoon she said that she would talk to father about all this but that I "shouldn't get my hopes up".

My life is down the drain, flushed all the way to Jacksonville.

I wish that we still lived with Grandpa and Grandma Kent. I was just a little girl back then, but life was so much better. Dad was off fighting for our country in WWII. Nobody yelled or screamed at me or asked me to do anything other than be good and go to school. Father says that Grandpa Lester is "backward" because he can't read. So what if he can't read? Grandma Mary reads for him. He sure knows how to work, how to make those mules obey without a whip! Grandpa never went bankrupt either. I think my father might be the one who is backward.

The only two places I've ever lived have been at Grandpa's house and here.

Jacksonville is a big city. I don't think I'll like the big city. Will all the kids at my new school hate me, call me a "hick from the sticks" and generally give me hell? Can I still play the piano? Why do I have to try and figure all this out; my life was all figured out.

Maybe I shouldn't be angry. Vince and Luke are going to need me, that's for sure.

Especially if mom is working every day, all day long. I do love my brothers very much.

Aunt Mabel would love to have me live with her while I finish school. We get along so well, Aunt Mabel and me. It's probably because she is not from the South, she's from Austria. She talks with a funny accent, although she says we have the funny accents. Uncle Porter married her over there in Europe when he was fighting the war against the Germans. I love the story about how they met.

One day Uncle Porter's army unit rolled into Leoben, Austria. The war had only been over for a few days. Most of the Austrians were happy to see the Americans, but Uncle Porter said that some of them supported Hitler and hated the U.S. "You had to be careful," he always said when he told this part of the story. "Never could be sure if an Austrian wanted to hug you or shoot you."

A buddy told Uncle Porter about this gorgeous Austrian girl who worked in a tiny little clothing store on the outskirts of town. While the duds were nothing special, the Austrian girl sure was, according his friend. So Uncle Porter went to the little store.

Mabel was a stunner, that's for sure. I've seen pictures of her back then and it wasn't that long ago when all this happened. My Aunt Mabel is looker, everyone says so. Maybe that's another reason why we get along so well because I'm a looker too.

Anyway, Uncle Porter says he fell in love with Aunt Mabel right then and there.

Now, I'm not sure it ever happens like that, but it makes for a good story. What is for sure is that my uncle finagled it so that he could stay in the area after his unit pulled out because he was so smitten. He courted Aunt Mabel proper, treated her like a queen.

Even went to her father's house to ask for her hand in marriage. Mabel says she was smitten too, if for no other reason than my uncle was so determined.

They were the happiest couple I ever knew; always playing with each other—teasing, cuddling and laughing. My folks don't even seem to like each other half the time. Maybe they were like Porter and Mabel once; maybe they somehow forgot how much they love each other. I don't know, but I do know that when I get married I want to be like Porter and Mabel, happy and in love and right with the world.

A couple of years ago Uncle Porter was standing in the wrong place at the wrong time at a big construction site up in Columbia, South Carolina. A piece of steel fell right on him, killing him instantly. Aunt Mabel was torn up, completely heartbroken. For a few weeks she didn't talk to anybody or see anybody or do anything. I thought she might die too, from the grief.

It was the saddest thing I've ever been through. I felt so bad, I love Mabel so much, but there was nothing I could do to help her. I felt powerless, a lot like I feel right now.

"Honey," Mother calls. "Supper's on. Your brothers are out back somewhere.

Please make sure Luke and Vince wash up before dinner."

"Yes ma'am."

Our little house has a really nice back yard; two peach trees, a walnut tree and an oak and just about a million flowers. Go out the back gate and you are in little brother paradise, as I call it, open land all the way to the canal. Those boys love to play cowboys and Indians, build forts and run around out there until last light.

Dad has never really connected with Luke. He was off fighting the war when he was born and the two of them definitely don't mesh. Whatever Luke does, it's never good enough. I don't get it and I think its plain mean. Luke has his hands full just being a twelve year old kid without having to put up with a father who is constantly making him feel lower than a slug.

My father has opinions on just about everything—the way things should be according to him. Sometimes I think that he could care less about how anyone else feels about anything, as if he was the only one in the world who mattered.

Little Vince worships his older brother so, in a way, that sort of makes up for my father's nonsense. If he'd let him, Vince would follow Luke around all day long, every day like my dog Kraus follows me. I give him full credit; Luke has the patience of Job. Not many twelve year olds would put up with a little brat, almost four year old brother tugging at them from sunup to sundown.

"Luke! Vince! Supper!" If I yell, sooner rather than later my brothers come running. They know the penalty for not coming straight home when called, a smack on the backside with my father's leather belt.

Tonight we're having ham, a rare treat. I think my father is trying to make up for giving us the bad news last night. It won't work with me. I'm still steaming, but I know better than to mouth off at the dinner table.

My father arrives right on time, my brothers charge in a second later. Typical Thursday at our house, but I suppose our whole schedule changes after this week.

Everything changes after this week.

"Bless this food that we are about to consume, let it nourish and strengthen our bodies oh Lord. Amen." Father always says grace before supper and it's always the same short prayer too.

"I got the job for sure at the ship yard," Mom announces. "Just like that? How'd ya pull that off so fast?"

"It's only solid for six months and they need workers, especially bookkeepers."

"Dad," I say, interrupting.

"I'm not finished talking with your mom yet, Sonja. Mind your manners." Father returns his attention to my mother. "Same pay as they were talkin' 'bout last week?"

"Ten dollars more a month."

"What a blessing," Dad says in a mocking tone.

A minute or so passes, no one says a word. I know the drill. I will be told when I am allowed to talk.

"Go ahead, Sonja."

"Did you speak with Aunt Mabel today?"

"I did. I called her on my lunch hour."

"Did she ask you if …"

"You ain't stayin' here, Sonja. Mabel ain't the issue. I know she would look after you proper. We need you with us, ain't I made that plain enough? Your mother is goin' to hafta work full time, maybe more. You need to look after your brothers."

"I don't need much lookin' after pa and I can tend to Vince," Luke offers, knowing that he was risking punishment for speaking out of turn.

The volcano is about to blow, I can see it in his eyes. I want to run, but having tried that before I know that will only make things worse.

"Why the hell should I have to listen to this nonsense in my own home?" Father yells, as he pounds his fist on the table. "I work like a damn slave to provide for this family and all I get in return is bitchin' and moanin'! Can't a man eat his supper in peace?"

One more word from any of us and we all know what will happen next, father will break out the strap. So the rest of the meal passes by in a tense silence until my father finishes eating, gets up from the table and walks out onto the front porch to have a smoke.

CHAPTER TWO

Miss Andrea Bloom's home is on the other side of town. It takes me an hour on the bus to get there, but it's well worth the effort. Of all of the things that I will miss about Augusta, piano lessons from Miss Bloom are at the top of the list.

"Hello child," Miss Bloom says as she greets me at the door. Her house smells good, like potpourri and fresh baked cookies. Everything is always in such perfect order. I'm sure that she must have a maid who goes around and straightens up every hour. Not so much as a throw pillow is ever out of place.

"Last lesson?" Miss Bloom asks, already knowing the answer.

"Yes," I reply, trying not to cry. "On Monday we're moving to Jacksonville."

"Your mamma told me, just wanted to be sure. Are you going to keep up with your lessons in Florida?"

"I'll try." I don't like to lie, but a fib seems called for at the moment. My father has made it plain as day that we don't have the money anymore for "luxuries" like piano lessons. I do not want to disappoint Miss Bloom, either.

"What about your scholarship? Can you still qualify?"

"No, I'm afraid not. I'm just going to have to …" It is too much. I promised myself that I wouldn't break down, but I can't keep it all bottled up inside me for even one more second.

"There, there, honey," Miss Bloom says, as she puts her arm around me and pats me on the back. "You let it all out dear. Maybe we should just talk today rather than play. It might do you more good."

"My life is over," I pronounce between sobs.

"It may seem that way child, but your life hasn't even started yet. Worse things will happen to you before it's done than having to move to another city. But I understand, you don't want to leave Augusta."

"I hate my father."

"No you don't, Sonja. I know you don't."

"Yes I do. This mess is all his fault."

"That may be true, but you still don't hate your father."

"Right now, I hate him."

"Can I tell you a story?"

"Sure."

"First let's have a cup of tea."

Miss Bloom has the most wonderful silver tea set. After my lesson, if there was time, she would often make tea and we would take it on her screened porch. Whenever she serves tea to me in her beautiful bone china cups I feel like a princess, a real English lady.

I really want some tea today. I really need some of Miss Bloom's wisdom.

"You know, I haven't always been Miss Bloom," she announces, as she brings in the tea and sets it down on the small table in front of her wicker couch. "I was married once for a short time."

I had no idea. Neither did anyone else. Daddy calls Miss Bloom "that old spinster" and I always thought what he meant by that was Miss Bloom never had a husband or children.

"What happened?" I ask as I delicately bring the cup to my lips and sip the tea, just like a real cultured girl.

"Back in 1940 we actually had a hurricane in Georgia. I know, they don't move up here too often, but this storm came in fast with no warning. My Tommy, that was my husband's name, he was trying his best to get any old job anywhere to make as much money as he could. We all knew that the war would come to us soon enough. The Yankees were already starting to draft boys."

Miss Bloom always referred to the government as "the Yankees". Like many people I know who are a generation or two older than me, the wounds from the war that ended ninety years ago are still fresh.

"It wasn't a dangerous job; all he had to do was deliver supplies to some warehouse. He was loading and unloading trucks. Now, my Tommy wanted much more out of life. He's the one who taught me how to play the piano. You know those beautiful sonatas you love so much? Tommy wrote them."

"I thought Beethoven or Bach or Mozart wrote those pieces."

"Nope. Thomas Shaw of Augusta, Georgia composed that music."

"Have you ever shown them to, I don't know, an orchestra leader or something?"

"No one will ever play those pieces except for me and my most special students."

I blush. Very daintily I take a nibble from one of Miss Bloom's shortbread cookies.

"Anyway, Tommy and I were saving money as fast as we could because we thought for sure that he would get called up and I would be stuck here for a while on my own. He had a brother down in Savannah, so when a job came open down that way, Tommy hopped in his old Studebaker and worked for a few days."

"He was just driving down the road when the wind and the rain started. He was hauling a full load, too much weight as I later learned. He turned a corner too sharp and got a full blast of water and wind right off the river. His truck spun out of control, tipped over and he was killed."

Just like Mabel and Porter! I scream in my mind. I hope my true love doesn't die!

Why do such things happen to good people? "What did you do?"

"I went on, honey. It's what we all do, go on. I never met another man that could hold a candle to Tommy Shaw. Oh I dated more than a few, especially right after the war. All those boys came back looking for a bride. But I never really came close to marrying any of them. I figured that the memory of Tommy would fade, that I would stop missing him, that another man could make me feel like he made me feel. But, wasn't to be. That's why I live alone and I never re-married. I went back to using the name Miss Bloom because I didn't want people thinking of me as some poor widow who lived with twenty cats and played piano all day in a house with all the shades drawn."

"Aren't you," I want to say the right thing, not offend. "Lonely, Miss Bloom?"

"I miss Tommy every minute, child. But I have my students and my dear friends and this lovely home. My life is full. Not complete, but full."

"I'd be mad if I were you. Mad at God, mad at the storm, mad at..."

Miss Bloom reaches over and gently touches my hand. "That's what I'm trying to tell you, child. Being angry does no good, no good at all. Hate does you no good, it's just another way of being angry. You have to let all of it go, do what the Good Book says and forgive. I forgave the storm and the war and the circumstances. I even forgave God, although I know that sounds like blasphemy, but I needed to make some peace with Him. Someday Tommy and I will be together and no storm or war or anything will be able to keep us apart."

"I hear what you're saying, Miss Bloom."

"Do ya? I want you to hear with your heart, child. Having to pull up stakes and move to Jacksonville is not the end of the world. You're a beautiful girl. I'll just bet that your true love is waiting down there for you right now. He will sweep you off your feet, love you always and buy you a piano. You just wait and see."

"I hope you're right."

"Have I ever been wrong?" Miss Bloom asks in her piano teacher voice. "No ma'am," I answer, as a dutiful student.

"Would you like to play one of Tommy's pieces that I've never shown you? It's actually my favorite."

"Would I! Yes, Miss Bloom, but I would be taking more than my hour. I don't have any more …"

"I'm not accepting any money from you today, Sonja. I want you to keep the two dollars your mom gave you for my fee; you'll need it in Jacksonville. Today we are just two friends playing piano on a rainy day."

Miss Bloom calls my mother and tells her that I will not be home until five. We play Tommy's piece, it's lovely. She gives me the sheet music for it after I swear on the Bible that I will never show it to another living soul.

When I leave Miss Bloom's house I feel alive again, full of joy. Music has that effect on me, it perks me right up when I'm feeling down or, like today, sorry for myself. On the bus ride home I think all about Mabel and Porter and Miss Bloom and Tommy. I want what they had, a true love who will treat me like I am the most special thing God ever created. Only he can't die and leave me miserable! I beg God not to let that happen to me.

CHAPTER THREE

"I halfta pee, mamma."
"For heaven's sakes Jerry, pull over. Vince is gonna explode."
"We just stopped thirty miles ago. He shoulda peed then."
"He's three, Jerry. Pull over."
"For the love of Pete. We'll never get there at this rate."
Father jerks the car off of the main road and stops behind a small group of trees.
Since I'm in the back seat with my brothers, the duty falls on me to take Vince to an appropriate spot out of public view so that he can relieve himself.
"Don't dawdle," Daddy warns as he steps outside of the car for a smoke.
Luke and Kraus come along too. We all want out of the steam bath that is the backseat of Dad's Chevy. August in Florida is not very pleasant; ninety degrees and ninety percent humidity. None of the rest of us has to pee because any moisture we consume is sweated out real quick.
"How much longer, sis?" Luke asks me because he knows better than to ask father.

"An hour or so, I guess. We're about fifty miles away by my calculations." I have my own map so I can keep track of things.

"I hope the moving guys got all of my stuff."

"That's their job, Luke. They got all of your stuff."

"Dad threw away a lot."

"What besides your old comic books?"

"My bug collection and my dead frogs."

For once I'm on Dad's side. "They'll be plenty of bugs and frogs in Jacksonville.

You needed a new collection anyway."

"I do wanna go to the beach. Will you come with me?"

"Sure, we'll take Vince too."

"Do we have to?"

"Not always. I'll go just with you sometimes."

"Okay."

"Hey, is Vince done doin' his business yet? We're burnin' daylight here!" Father has such a way with words.

"Coming!" I yell back.

"Feel better?" I ask little Vince as he emerges from the bush, buttoning up his fly. "Yea. Thanks, sis. No more soda pop."

"Not 'til we get there. You can sip water."

We pile back into our rolling torture chamber. Kraus has to have the window seat next to me so he can hang his head out as we drive. We make quite a sight driving down the highway—a family of five in a forty nine Chevy pulling a trailer with a German Shepard flapping in the breeze. Last semester we read Steinbeck's *The Grapes Of Wrath* in English class. I imagine that is what we look like, a Georgian version of the Joads traveling down the road in our jalopy, heading away from trouble and toward an uncertain future.

I smell the ocean first. As the countryside ends the salt marshes begin. The heat only gets worse the closer we get to Jacksonville. We cross a bridge, go over what I figure is some kind of river or inlet. I'm too tired to follow along on my map anymore; I know that we are headed south on Highway Nine, that's enough. I just want the whole ordeal to be over. Vince has to pee again, Luke is getting antsy and Kraus is about ready to jump out of the window and start running beside the car.

Father's map leads him directly to our new house. The place isn't as bad as I had imagined it would be. It has a decent front yard and a paved driveway. By the time we pull in at almost nine pm I would have been happy to flop in a deserted building for the night as long as I could get the you know what out of that car.

My room is in the back of the place, next to mom and dad's. Vince and Luke have to share a room that is much smaller than the one they shared in Augusta. I guess whoever Dad is renting the place from knew that we were coming. Our furniture won't arrive until morning, but some kind soul has put sleeping bags with pads under them in each room. They even made a pot of stew and it is waiting for us in the fridge along with some bread, butter and jam.

Mom heats up the stew on her new stove which, I have to admit, is a step up from the old burner she struggled with in Augusta. We eat in silence because we are dog tired. Mom takes a shower. Even though it is pitch black outside, Luke and Vince take a peek at their new back yard.

I take off my sweat drenched clothes, throw on an old shirt and collapse into my sleeping bag.

Hallelujah. I made it to Jacksonville alive.

I'm so glad it's September. I'm ready to go back to school. Everything has changed, and not for the better.

I haven't touched a piano in over a month, not since that wonderful afternoon at Miss Bloom's house. My mind, my soul, just isn't right unless I can play. There is something so soothing, so re-assuring about playing the piano. Now, I know that most kids have to be dragged kicking and screaming to their piano lessons, like they were going to the dentist or something. For me, it's just the opposite; when my music is taken from me, my spirit sags. I can't help it.

Of course my father has no sympathy for me whatsoever. I don't think he really cares about anybody but himself. That is a really mean thing to say, I know, but what's the use in hiding from the truth? It's not like the truth is going to change if you don't talk about it or go away if you pretend it isn't there. The more I find out about this whole bankruptcy thing the less sympathy I have for him, that's for sure.

A week ago I was sent to the store on a Saturday afternoon to fetch some groceries. Dad wasn't home when I left; he was working at some odd job down at the ship yard. By the time I got back with a sack full of food, Dad had the house to himself. I put away the groceries and went to my room to lie down. I heard my father talking on the phone in his bedroom. He had left his bedroom door open, probably because it was so dang hot and because he had not heard me come in.

He was arguing with someone. Nothing unusual about that, my dad argues with a lot of people. After a few minutes I figured out that he was talking to Jeff, who is his best bosom buddy from the Army and lives in Cleveland or somewhere. Mom told me once that father tells Jeff everything – a whole lot more than he ever tells her, that's for sure.

I couldn't believe what I was hearing, so I sat real still and concentrated. After a few minutes I was sure—sure that my father was a damn fool.

Jeff was trying to tell my dad that he, how can I put this and not offend, should remove his head from his derriere. The bankruptcy law is pretty clear, is what I gathered.

The reason the law exists is so that people can get out from under their debts without killing themselves or their families. The law says that you can "discharge" your debts, get rid of your debts, the money you owe people, by going to court. Dad was repeating these words to his friend because his friend was making sure that he understood what was what. Dad understood alright, he just disagreed.

My father's pride would not allow him to use the law of the land to settle his affairs. He would rather force our whole family to leave the home we love, to force mom to get a full time job, to put himself through hell by working like a dog six or seven days a week than admit that he had made some mistakes running the lumber yard. The worst thing in the world to my father was owing a dime to anybody. I guess I better not say that was the "worst thing" because the worst thing in the world to him was someone talking crap about him.

I laid there in my bed just dumfounded. All my father had to do was go to court and let the judge deal with the bank? It's not as if he owed money to family or friends, I knew that much already. He had borrowed money from the bank for the lumber yard and when it went broke he couldn't pay it back. I figure about a million people must have been in the same predicament at one time or another. I could tell Jeff felt the same way and he was trying to talk some sense into my father.

I wondered if he'd told Mom all this. What if she didn't know? Would it matter if she did? I'll bet Aunt Mabel knew, that's for sure. When I really thought about it I said to myself, heck everyone must know! The law is the law; it doesn't change from person to person.

My father probably did not stop and consider that all those people who he was so afraid would say bad things about him behind his back if he "discharged" his debts were probably getting a belly laugh at his expense because he was the only fool in the world who would worry about paying back a debt to a bank when the bankruptcy court could get rid of it.

Now, I'm not saying that paying what you owe is not the way to live. From what I gathered, that's not what Jeff was saying either. Sometimes people just get in over their heads and bad things happen. Jeff pretty much felt this is what happened to Dad. In that situation it's time to swallow your pride, take the consequences and move on.

But no. I had to lose my scholarship and my piano and Mom had to go to work.

Banks are built to handle bad times. Even I know they build losses into their loan calculations so they don't go broke when payments aren't made. That's just business.

So all this time I had figured that Dad just got caught in a bad situation with no way out.

But there was a way out, he just wouldn't take it. I'd call that just plain ignorant.

Ignorant or not I cannot let this whole mess consume me. I talked with Aunt Mabel on the phone yesterday and, like I thought, she knew all about the bankruptcy situation. She reminded me that soon enough I'd be grown and making my own decisions. If my father chose to handle things his way that was his choice, not mine.

She was right, of course. I vowed to just let it be from here on out, to not think about it or worry about it. What was done is done. I live in Jacksonville and I have to help take care of my two brothers for a couple of more years. That's the way it is.

There is one ray of light in my gloom. Father talked with Reverend Walker over at the First Baptist Church. They need someone to play piano for them during the service and a couple of times during the week. I should be able to sneak in some private time for myself on the piano working around their schedule.

I'm cheered up, at least as much as I can be. I hope the kids are nice at my new school but, whether they're nice or not, at least I won't have to spend all day around here doing chores and feeling sorry for myself.

CHAPTER FOUR

There are only two white high schools in Jacksonville, Andrew Jackson and Robert E. Lee. From what some of the girls in my new neighborhood tell me, I'm lucky to be going to Jackson. I guess the schools are big rivals. I'll bet that if I was headed to Lee all the kids there would say how lucky I was to be going to Lee. School spirit and all that, I suppose.

There is a school bus stop right down the block from our house. In Augusta all the kids took the same bus, whether you went to elementary, middle school or high school. But here in Jacksonville the high school kids have their own bus. Luke was not very happy about that, but I sure was. I love my little brother, but it will be really nice not to have him tugging at my skirt on the first day. Probably better for him too. He needs a fresh start and hiding behind me rather than mixing it up with the boys on the bus is probably not what's best for him.

Aunt Mabel made me the most beautiful dress to wear on my first day of school. In the letter she sent with the dress she explained how she had researched all the latest fashions and sent for a pattern from New York for a *Christian Dior* dress she said would make me look "gorgeous". It is the nicest dress I've ever owned, that's for sure.

It has a floral print and two straps that tie on top. My shoulders are bare. Mabel even sent along a string of imitation pearls for me to wear with the outfit.

I look like a million bucks. I wonder if I look too good. Just my luck and all the other kids will be dressed down for school. I have this brief nightmare of me walking into class dressed to the nines and everyone erupting in laughter because I look like I'm going to church or the prom or something.

Dad doesn't like my dress, not one bit. He stops short of ordering me not to wear it because he can tell this is one of the few times my mother would likely step up and say something to him.

"Tryin' to attract some attention?" he rudely asks me at the breakfast table, as if I'm a floozy or something.

"It's a new style, Dad. Aunt Mabel made it for me. You know, I told you."

"Just because…" My father stops talking, because mother gives him a stare that could melt steel. "It's too much for a girl. You're not a movie star, you're a kid. I gotta go."

"You look very nice, Sonja," Mother compliments right after Dad leaves. "Did you send your aunt a thank you note for making the dress for you?"

"Yes ma'am."

"Off you go then. Keep your chin up. First days are hard, I know. I had a few in my life."

First days at school aren't hard, they're dreadful.

I discover that my stop must be near the end of the line because the bus is packed when I get on. Nearly all of the seats are full and everyone is talking. I don't know anyone. The only other students I'd met in my neighborhood are all driven to school by their parents.

Some of the boys are giving me the once over. I like that and try to put a smile on my face. One girl scowls as I pass by but she makes a face at me for the right reason, because the boy sitting next to her was noticing me. So far, so good.

I sit in the back next to a girl with bad skin and big, black glasses. We say hi to each other and that's about it. Someone has a transistor radio blaring in the front and I can hear the Platters singing, "*Only You*". I love that song; it always makes me think about my dream guy and how much he will love me and be totally devoted and all that. I spend the next fifteen minutes lost in a pleasant fog trying to figure out which boy on the bus likes me the most.

Classes go by without a hitch. Everyone was at least polite and in one class a couple of the boys stared at me and passed notes. My dress is a hit, thank God. I'm not expecting to meet my new best friend or the love of my life on the first day of school, just survive.

I brought my lunch, which tells everyone that I'm a poor kid. The students with a few nickels in their pockets buy the hot lunch they serve in the cafeteria. I sit down in the cafeteria at the end of the table and open up my tomato sandwich, which is my very favorite. The school can keep their hot lunches for all I care.

"Hi," the pretty, black haired girl says as she sits down next to me. "I'm Carol."

"Sonja," I respond, trying my best to be friendly.

"Are you new here?"

"We just moved to Jacksonville last month from Augusta."

"Love your dress."

"Thank you."

"Did you make it?"

"No, my aunt did."

"She must be a professional," Carol pronounces as she opens her sack lunch and takes a bite of her sandwich.

"Are you new too?" I ask.

"Sorta. We moved here last spring. My Dad's in the Navy."

"Do you like it, the school I mean?"

"Not as much as my old school in San Diego. I miss California."

"I miss Augusta."

"Then we have something in common," Carol declares. "We have to make the best of things, don't we?"

"Seems like," I say. "You sure…"

Our pleasant conversation is rudely interrupted by two boisterous girls who slam down their trays and sit down across the table across from us. They are fast talkers who say a whole lot about nothing over and over again. I know the type quite well—

girls without a brain in their heads and only one concern; who was saying what about whom.

Gossips. I don't like gossips.

"Hey," the cute, petite one says, looking over at us. "Hey," Carol and I respond.

"Elvis said he's coming back," the other one says. She is a red head, quite tall and very shapely.

"Didn't know he was ever here," I offer.

"Where do you live? On the moon? You didn't go down to the theater for the show last May?" the petite girl shouts.

"She's new," Carol clarifies, coming to my rescue. "Sonja just moved here from Augusta a month ago."

"Well then let me tell you *all* about it," the redhead says, as if she had just been given the opportunity of a lifetime. "Elvis, that dreamboat, did a show in Jacksonville last May. Everybody's been talking about nothing else *all* summer."

What a shame, I think, but don't say. There has to be something better to talk about for three months than Elvis Presley. Maybe not if you're a flighty nitwit.

"Carter gave me this picture. His dad works at the paper. Can you believe it?

Elvis without his shirt on." The redhead hands me the picture.

"Nice," I politely respond. I'm not impressed. Elvis is good looking, but I don't get why all the girls think he is the greatest thing since sliced bread. I return the picture. "Pastor Gray says it's indecent," the petite girl states with authority. "They were going to print the picture in the paper, to show what happened to him that night, but the Pastor put a stop to it."

"It's just a boy with his shirt off. You can see the same thing at the beach every day of the week," I opine.

"I wish Elvis was at the beach every day of the week," the redhead moans. "Judge Gooding told Elvis that he had to clean up his act. If he comes back to Jacksonville and moves his hips, you know, the *way* he does, the Judge said he would throw him jail." The petite girl has a face like a chipmunk and teeth to match. When she says this my first thought is to offer her an acorn or a walnut.

"You think that's funny?" the redhead asks, clearly annoyed.

"No", I say, still grinning because I'm unable to get the vision of a furry rodent out of my head. "I think Elvis is a great dancer. I love to dance."

"Let's go, Carrie," the petite chipmunk says. "We need to check our lockers before the bell rings."

Clearly I've offended the bubble head Bobbsey twins. "Friends of yours?" I ask Carol after the girls depart. "I thought they were your friends."

We laugh. I had made a pal on my first day of school. As it turns out, the first day wasn't so dreadful after all.

CHAPTER FIVE

I wish the church was closer to our house. It took me nearly as long to get here on the bus as it used to take me to get to Ms. Bloom's, dang near an hour. I want my piano to be in my living room, like it used to be. But I promised myself not to live in the past.

Dad sold my piano to pay back the bank. I try not to think about it too much, but it's hard. I was used to getting up in the morning and playing before school and then playing some after school. My mom and brothers loved it when I'd play – I filled the house with music and joy.

Our house isn't the same anymore. Heck, our house is gone.

Now I'm standing in front of this little Baptist church praying that God has a piano inside that He will let me play.

The building is nice, all white with a cross on top. It's not a big place – I imagine they could cram a hundred souls in here on Sunday if they filled every seat.

"You must be Sonja," the pastor says, as he walks over to me and shakes my hand. "I'm Reverend Walker, Peter Walker."

"Reverend," I answer. "Nice to meet you."

"Your father told me that you're quite the musician."

"I don't know about that, Reverend," I respond demurely. "But I can play the piano."

"Well, we sure need you, Sonja. Walter has the choir in shape, but the hymns just don't sound the same without a piano."

"Walter?"

"Walter Barker. You don't know him? He goes to Andrew Jackson. I think he's a Junior. Are you a Senior?"

"Nope, I'm a Junior too."

"I think the two of you will get along just fine."

"I'm sure we will."

"Would you like to see the piano?"

Would I, I shout in my mind. The Reverend is nice and all and I know that this is probably going to be our church home from now on, but I didn't come here to chit chat, I came to play.

It isn't any great shakes, but Baldwin pianos are generally good quality instruments that last forever if they are regularly tuned and properly cared for. I wonder what kind of shape it's in.

"Has it been tuned recently?" I ask.

"Yesterday. As soon as I knew that we had a new piano player I called the folks down at Harveys and they came right over and tuned her up. Give her a spin, Sonja."

I brought along a small collection of sheet music. I have been dying to play Miss Bloom's favorite piece again, the one we played together right before I moved.

The keys feel so good beneath my fingers. As I begin to play I settle into that wonderful bliss of total concentration and complete peace, the way I always feel when I am absorbed in music. While I stumble once or twice because I'm a bit rusty, no one would have noticed but me.

"That was lovely, Sonja. I didn't recognize that hymn. Is it new?"

"Oh, that wasn't a hymn, Reverend. It was a sonata. It was written by my piano teacher's husband who was a very talented…"

"Could you play me a hymn, Sonja? We need you to play hymns for us here at the church."

I almost open my big mouth and say the wrong thing. It must have been the Good Lord who clamped it shut. Thank you, Jesus.

The last thing I need to do is offend the man who just might give me access to a decent piano.

"Sure, Pastor. Do you have one in mind that you'd like to hear?"

"How about, '*All Creatures of Our God and King*'. I know that Walter has the sheet music around here…"

I interrupt the Reverend by playing the song. I know it, and many other Baptist hymns, by heart.

"Impressive! You are answered prayer, young lady."

"Would you like to hear another one?"

"*How Great Thou Art?*"

Talk about simple. I play the piece flawlessly.

"Absolutely fantastic, Sonja. Welcome to the First Baptist Church family."

"Thank you."

"Are you available for services on Sunday? We have two services, one at nine and another at eleven-thirty."

"Yes, of course."

"On Saturdays the choir practices from nine to eleven. Would you be available then as well?"

"I'll be there, Reverend. Every week."

"It's settled then."

"Are there times when I could come in and play, during the week I mean, when I wouldn't be disturbing anyone?"

"Let's see…sure. There is no one around Monday or Tuesday night or after choir practice on Saturday. I'll give you a key. You can let yourself in and out. Just be sure to lock up."

Thank you Jesus, I say in my mind. Thank you, thank you, thank you.

"That would be wonderful," I respond, trying not to sound overly enthusiastic. "I'll be right back," Pastor Walker says as he gets up and walks out a door that leads, I assume, to his office.

I see what has to be the choir director's box sitting nearby. I look inside. Most of the hymns they're singing I'm already very familiar with so I will not have to practice them. The less time I have to spend on church music, the more I can spend on my own.

There is a picture in the box of the choir. The young man in the front has to be Walter. I have seen him before. All I know about him is that he is a basketball player. Odd combination, I think to myself, basketball player and church choir director.

Pastor Walker returns holding a key.

"Here you go, Sonja," he says. "Please come in and out the side door." He points at the particular door I am to use.

"Understood, sir."

"Well, I'm off. Mrs. Parsons is in the hospital again, poor dear. Gallstones, I'm afraid."

"Oh my," I empathize.

"No reason why you can't stay a while and play, Sonja. No one will be needing the church until Bible study at seven."

"I'll be gone by six thirty."

"Enjoy yourself, young lady." The Pastor turns to leave, then hesitates and stops. "This is a house of God, Sonja. The sonata you played was fine – anything like that is appropriate. Even though you are alone in here with no one but the Lord listening, please do not play any of that new rock and roll stuff or something offensive. Are we in agreement?"

"Yes, Pastor. I will behave myself."

"Very good. God bless."

Things are generally looking up. I have access to a decent piano. I have a new friend who I really like. School is okay. Maybe I'll make it in Jacksonville after all.

On general principles I bang out *"Ain't That a Shame"* by Fats Domino as soon as I'm sure that I'm alone.

God understands, I'm not offending Him.

Men who believe that they have some God given right to tell me what to do, think or play, now that's offensive.

CHAPTER SIX

"Is this where we go?" I ask Carol, who is leading the way to the first day of band practice.

"Yep, back of the gym. Mr. Porter was very clear about that."

"Is the band any good?" I need to know.

"Fair to middlin'. You're the best musician in the school, Sonja. Don't expect any of us to be up to your speed."

"I just hope that we can carry a tune, that's all."

"Mr. Porter is, well, a bit loud, Sonja."

"Loud?"

"He likes to scream a lot."

Lord have mercy, I silently say to myself. A man like my father that is what I immediately envision.

A very unpleasant prospect, to say the least.

"My career in the Andrew Jackson High School band might not be a long one then, Carol. Dealing with another yelling …"

"Give him a chance, Sonja."

Carol and I have become close friends very quickly. Unlike almost every other girl in school, Carol is not from the South. She was raised on a series of Navy bases and has lived for a time in many places—from Seattle to New Hampshire to San Diego and now here in Jacksonville.

She loves California. The first thing you learn when you become Carol's friend is that the sun rises and sets on Southern California. She intends to move back there as soon as possible after graduation. To do exactly what does not matter to her, she just knows that California is home and home is where she wants to be.

I definitely feel less sorry for myself about having to move to Jacksonville after getting to know Carol. For her entire life every two or three years she has been uprooted. Her father is a very nice and loving person and I can tell that he and Carol are close.

What a blessing, I told her, to have a father like that. Her mother dropped out of her life when she was a baby and she has not seen her since. Carol was never sure why other than her mother met another man and said goodbye to her and her dad permanently.

"Okay, okay, welcome," Mr. Porter screams through his megaphone. There is no need to yell. There are only thirty of us at the meeting and we are all within twenty feet of Mr. Porter.

"See what I mean," Carol whispers in my ear.

I did. This type of yelling I can deal with, no problem. Annoying, but no problem.

"My name is Mr. Porter and I will be your faculty band leader. I know most of you, but if you weren't in band last year, please tell me your name and what instrument you play."

I wait my turn. There are only a few new kids.

"Sonja Kent," I say, deliberately using a soft voice. "I can play many different instruments."

"What can you play?" Mr. Porter is still using his megaphone even though I'm standing ten feet from him.

"The oboe, clarinet and percussion," I answer in a matter of fact tone. "Really?," Mr. Porter responds, incredulously.

"Yes sir."

"We really need us a snare drummer and someone who can play percussion instruments like bells and cymbals. Can you do that for us?"

"Yes sir. No problem."

"Great then. We meet here for third period every day. Has everyone got band on their schedule?"

No one spoke up, so Mr. Porter assumed that everyone did.

"Great then. Be sure to bring your band fees with you next week when you come to class. We've kept it down to ten dollars this year; more donations from the community. That is all."

"Fees?" I ask Carol.

"Yep. It costs ten dollars a year for us to be in the band. It pays for our uniforms and other stuff. You didn't know?"

"No. Band was free back in Augusta."

"Sonja, if that's a problem for you I can ask my dad if …"

"No, it's not a problem." I quickly change the subject. "Hey, let's go down to Ozzies tonight. I'll teach you how to play pinball."

"It's a deal! When can you get there?"

"By six. I have to make dinner and do some other chores first."

"Should I ask him?"

"That's not a good idea, honey."

"Then I guess I won't do band this year, Mom. It's okay; it's not the end of the world."

"How much was it again?"

"Ten dollars."

My mother digs into her purse, looks at her wallet, thinks better of it and closes her handbag. Then she says to me, "You never saw this."

Mother gets down on all fours in front of the sink. She reaches way into the back. I can hear things jostling around. She pulls out an old can of cleanser. The top has been cut off and slid back on. She opens it and pulls out a small wad of bills.

"This is my secret little stash, Sonja. Please don't ever tell your father about it." From the looks of it there is over a hundred dollars in the can, mostly in the form of five and ten dollar bills. She hands me a ten dollar bill.

"Will this cover your band fees?"

"Yes, Mom. Thank you so much, I really …"

She hands me another five dollar bill. "This is for you. Just because."

"Mom, I don't need it, you keep it."

"This little pile is for us, Sonja. So I don't have to go begging your father for money every time one of you children needs something."

I hug my mother and kiss her on the cheek. I know how hard she works for her pay. I feel like a heel asking her for more money right now.

Despite my vow to myself, I have to say something. It's been eating at me for far too long.

"Mom, I need to ask you something. Promise me that you won't get mad."

"Do you need more money?"

"No, it's not about money…well, it's about money, but not for me."

"Go ahead, honey."

"Did you know that Dad didn't have to pay back the bank? That he could have gotten rid of the whole mess through the court?"

"Of course I knew, Sonja."

"You're okay with that?"

"No, but he is my husband. It's not my place to tell him how to run our affairs."

"You give him all your money? Everything you make from your job?"

"Your father handles the money. As I just showed you, I hold a little back for special needs."

"Why? Why do you just go along with him all the time? I don't understand."

"It's not a woman's place to question her husband, Sonja."

"I don't believe that; no way, no how."

"C'mon now honey, some things are the way they are and there's not much sense in arguing about it. It's like trying to change the weather, can't be done."

"It's stupid. He's stupid."

"Mind your manners, Sonja. I love you, but don't get too familiar. Your father has earned our respect."

Shut up, Sonja, I say to myself. Apologize, be thankful and let it be. "Sorry. I can't see why he does the things he does sometimes."

"It isn't always our place to see, Sonja. Sometimes we just do what we have to do and move on."

We hug and kiss again. I finish my chores.

I love my mother very much. Faye Kent is a good woman and I am blessed to be her daughter. My father is beyond blessed to have her as his wife because most women simply would not bow to his every whim like he was a god or something.

Damn sure I never will. A man will never get the better of me and I wouldn't want to be married to anyone who thought it was okay to try.

CHAPTER SEVEN

Luke and I discovered Ozzies the second week or so after we arrived in Jacksonville. We needed a replacement for the Vincent's Drug Store back home, somewhere where they had a soda fountain and pinball machines and plenty of kids hanging out.

We didn't have any money for the soda fountain, but as long as there were pinball machines we didn't need any money. I am simply the greatest pinball player who everlived. Well, maybe not the greatest who ever lived, but I'd give the greatest a run for his money.

Ozzies has five pinball games, but my favorite is the Olympics machine. I swear I know that thing better than the people at Gottlieb who made her. I know how much you can disturb it without going tilt. I know when to hit this target, then the next one, then the next one and so on to I score the most points. It's an art form, it really is. Each machine has its own "feel" and the one in Ozzies is definitely loose, meaning I can bend it to my will without having to worry too much about losing a turn.

Mr. Kearns is the owner of Ozzies and he loves to see me coming through the door. Nothing draws 'em in like a pretty girl beating the daylights out of a pinball machine. I know it, he does too, so we made a deal. It was the same deal I had back in Augusta with the other guy – as long as I'm winning free games and racking up the points and drawing a crowd, I get sodas for free. I never drink more than one or two, so Mr. Kearns is getting a bargain. After about ten minutes or so I usually have ten people or more milling around the machine either cheering me on or hoping that I will drain the ball.

Carol wants to learn how to play. She has the spare nickels to try, that's for sure. My friend never hurts for money. While I wouldn't take advantage of a living soul, it's nice to have a girlfriend that isn't worried about spending a dime or two.

We're about half an hour into Carol's lesson when my meal ticket shows up. "You ladies look like you could use some instruction," the average looking boy says as he leans over the machine, trying his best to sound like James Dean. "Oh, that's alright, Sonja was …"

"Sure, we could use some help. Are you good at this?" Carol looks at me, almost opens her mouth, then just shuts up and smiles.

"I take to pinball like a duck takes to water ladies," the boy brags. "You're holdin' the flipper button all wrong, ah..what's your name?"

"Carol. My friend is Sonja."

"Sam, my friends call me Sammy."

"Show me how it's done, Sammy," Carol says.

Sammy isn't bad, but he's not red hot either. He is a slightly above average player who thinks he is a great player.

Sauce for the goose, as Grandpa Lester used to say.

After fifteen minutes of Carol enduring Sam's truly uninspiring lessons and polite flirting, I decide it's time.

"You're pretty good, Sammy," I say, speaking the literal truth. "I've played a time or two. What ya say you and I play a game."

"You're challenging *me* to a game?" There is a small crowd gathered around us now and, thankfully, none of them speak up and save Sam from his humility lesson.

"Unless you don't think that you can take a girl." This line is guaranteed to work every time.

"Do you have any money on you that you'd like to lose?"

"I'll back her," Carol says.

"Then let's go fifty cents. One game each, highest score wins."

"C'mon now. Fifty cents? I thought you were the greatest ever, Sammy. I've got five bucks in my pocket. Why don't you play for that?" Carol offers.

"Well, I don't know...lemme talk to my friends."

I whisper in Carol's ear. "You're pretty good at this. Do you think he'll bite for five bucks?"

"That's what he's doing over there right now, borrowing the money from his friends."

"This is like stealing," I say. "Oh, it's better than that, honey."

Sam returns, emboldened. "Okay, here's my five," he says, holding out five ones.

Carol reaches into her purse and pulls out a five dollar bill. "Who is gonna hold the money?"

"I will," Mr. Kearns says. I did not notice him before now, but he must have been watching the whole spectacle. I thought the jig might be up, but Mr. Kearns takes the money, stuffs it in his shirt pocket and winks at me once Sammy turns his head.

"Ladies first," Sam offers. "No, you go first. I insist."

Sam drops his nickel in the machine not knowing that the odds were far greater that the Good Lord would return in the next fifteen minutes than he would ever beat me in a game of pinball on my favorite machine.

As his buddies whoop and holler, Sam manages to complete a very respectable game earning two extra balls. He believes that his 500,000 point total is quite good. It isn't bad, but his score is far below my average on my worst day.

"Beat that, sister," Sam states smugly as his friends egg him on.

The crowd around the machine has grown now to over twenty kids. Some of them know me and understand the whole scheme.

"Hey freckle face," a boy from the crowd calls out to Sam. "Do ya know who P.T. Barnum was?"

"Yea," Sam answers, as he watches me pile up the points.

"Ya know what he said, don't ya? There's a sucker born every minute. He was talkin' 'bout you."

I can hear the laughter start, and the taunting and the "I told you that was her" comments.

Ten minutes later, with only two balls, I pass 500,000 points. There is no need to rub it in, so I let my last ball drain and declare victory.

"Thank you Sammy," I say. "Nice game."

"You hustled me."

"You hustled yourself," Mr. Kearns says, handing me the ten dollars.

Sam and his buddies tuck their tails between their legs and leave. I hear someone say that they go to Lee. I'm glad about that. Our exploits will make the rounds at school.

"Here," I say, giving Carol the money. "That was the most fun I've had since I don't know when."

"I'll keep my five, but Sam's money is yours. Hell, I'd have paid five bucks just to watch you whip his butt."

I guess I have to take back what I said about not taking advantage of another living soul.

If anyone, boy or girl, thinks that they can beat me on my favorite pinball machine, just let 'em try.

CHAPTER EIGHT

"Alright troops! Everyone at the ready!"

For once Mr. Porter's use of his megaphone is justified. The home crowd is on their feet and cheering. The first half is almost over. Our mighty Tigers are driving for a score with only seconds left on the clock.

"That's it!" Mr. Porter screeches as the second quarter ends. "On me now, let's go right into the fight song."

I love marching in the band. While percussion is not my favorite I understand that Mr. Porter needs a few kids who are versatile and I like being part of a team. The cymbals are easy to play. Since the steps are still a little new, I'm actually grateful tonight not to have to concentrate too much on my instrument.

Off we go and, for the most part, we are steady and true. The tunes are relatively easy, our fight song being the hardest. I'm not sure how closely anyone watches the band anyway. Most people are off to the concession stand or using the restroom, the band is killing time more than anything else. We really enjoy playing though and what would a Friday night football game be in the South without a marching band?

Disaster strikes as we are finishing our last number and heading back to the gym. What I remember before the pain and the blood started was being bumped by Billy Gorman. He plays the bass drum. He turned left when all the rest of us turned right. He made his mistake just as I was performing my final cymbal clash. He nearly toppled me and although I didn't fall, I did slash my thumb right above the joint on the cymbal. In a second my white glove was dark red from blood. I could feel that my thumb was barely still attached. Somehow I made it back to the gym.

"Carol," I say, about ready to pass out. "I think you need to get me to the hospital". Carol plays the trumpet in the band.

"What do you mean, honey…oh my Lord!"

Carol always drove her father's car to the football games. She did not hesitate, which was a good thing because I wasn't capable of doing much other than breathing. She screamed out for Mr. Porter, but he had left immediately after the band quit playing to find the principal.

We wrap my now totally blood soaked hand in a towel and off we run, moving as fast as we can toward her car.

Once we get in, Carol takes off like a race car driver.

"Slow down honey," I say, more than a bit woozy. "We have to make it to the hospital alive or it won't do us any good."

"Shush! Close your eyes and let me drive!"

Carol is focused and I am in no position to argue. The thought that keeps going through my head the most is how mad my father will be for having to pay the doctor bill.

I guess the police are occupied elsewhere, because somehow we arrive at the hospital without getting pulled over for speeding. Carol jumps out and leads me into the ER.

"My friend has cut off her thumb!" Carol yells. "Somebody help!"

Cooler heads soon prevail; it is a hospital after all. They put me in a wheelchair and roll me into a treatment room.

"Well hello there. Missing a thumb?" the doctor says, glibly. I like his sense of humor, but Carol is not amused.

"It's horrible! Wait 'til you see it!"

"Calm down young lady. If you would like to stay in here with your friend, I need you to sit down and let us do our work. Can you do that for me?"

"Yes sir," Carol answers, properly chastised. "Okay, well let's have a look see."

The doctor removes the towel, which is completely red now, not its original white. He tries to take off my glove, but it's stuck to my hand so he uses scissors and carefully cuts away the glove around my thumb.

I was right. Almost half the thumb has been severed. It's gross and bloody and too much for Carol.

She takes one look at my mangled thumb and passes out, gently slipping from her chair to the floor.

"I was afraid of that," the doctor says. "Nurse!" He and I are alone in the room together with Carol, the nurse had stepped out to get the proper bandages.

"Oh geez," the nurse says when she returns. She moves Carol on her back and when she does my friend wakes up. "That's enough excitement for one night, I suspect. Let's get you something to drink and take you out of here."

The doctor is busy with my thumb. He gave me a shot for the pain so I don't feel my hand at all.

"Sonja? I'm never sure if these charts are right."

"Yes, Sonja. Sonja Kent."

"How did this happen, Miss Kent?"

"A cymbal got in the way of my thumb."

"Your clothes are a dead giveaway. Is the cymbal alright?"

"No permanent damage." I really like this doctor.

"Well, I'm happy to say the same thing goes for your thumb. It'll hurt like the Dickens for a while, but you should be back playing the cymbals in a few weeks.

Perhaps you should consider switching to a safer instrument, Miss Kent."

"I will." The doctor is no more than thirty and quite good looking. There is no wedding ring on his hand. I'm smitten. For a second I actually consider slicing my other thumb just so he could fix that one too.

"Doctor," a different nurse says as she enters the room. "There is a Mr. Porter here from the school. He would like to speak with you about Miss Kent's injury."

"Certainly. Give me one more minute." The doctor is busy putting the finishing touches on my bandage. I'm busy naming our children. "There you go, Sonja. I'd shake your hand but, well…"

What a charmer! How about a kiss goodbye, I want to ask. But I don't, thank you Lord. "It was nice meeting you." I actually say that—"it was nice meeting you". Like we're at a party or something.

"It was nice meeting you too, Sonja."

Mr. Porter and Carol are waiting for me in the lobby. From the looks on their faces you'd have thought I had just cheated death. I'm in a fog, not because of my thumb, but because of the dreamy doctor who treated me.

"Are you okay?" Carol asks, giving me a strong hug.

"You might have to take notes for me in class for the next few days," I joke. "How about you? You dropped like a stone in there."

"I'm so embarrassed. I took one look at your hand and, well, I guess I'll never be a nurse."

"Are you alright, Miss Kent?" Mr. Porter actually says something to me without yelling. A first.

"I'm fine. I'll heal up in a few weeks according to the doctor."

"I'll go and see him now. The school is responsible for your injury, so I need to fill out some paperwork."

"The school will pay for the doctor?"

"Of course, you were injured during a school activity. That is why you pay your fees, Miss Kent."

Wow. Now I really wanted to get hurt again. If I could only be sure that he was on duty …

CHAPTER NINE

I can't go to the beach as much as the rest of the kids, but that doesn't bother me too much. My Saturday nights are usually free though and if there is a gathering down at Neptune Beach I am sure to go.

Neptune Beach is a small town, north of the big places. Jacksonville Beach is fine and all, but it has too much hustle-bustle for my taste. There are two really wonderful things about Neptune Beach – Nice House of Music and Silver's Drug Store.

Nice House of Music is a piano dealer and they have two or three floor models on display at all times. They also have the largest selection of sheet music in the area. They stay open late on Saturdays so I arrive around five or so and browse and dream about my future piano sitting in the living room of my future house.

Silver's Drug Store has two pinball machines. It's no Ozzies, but Silver's has its own particular charm. More than once I've spent the whole evening there playing pinball, missing the beach party entirely. Carol understands. Now that my thumb is healed and we had entered the new year of 1956, I am anxious to get back into shape. As good as I am at the game, I get rusty if I don't play pinball once or twice a week.

Tonight I skip the music store and Silver's and go straight to the beach. Carol is head over heels crazy about a boy, Rudy, who is a great football player. What is it about football players? The girls go nuts over 'em. I prefer basketball players myself, but that's just me.

I'm worried about my friend. Carol has a good head on her shoulders, but she can lose it real quick when it comes to boys. Now, I'm no perfect angel, but I've made up my mind that I am saving myself for my husband.

Aunt Mabel told me long ago that it was best remain a virgin until you're married. Grandma Mary said the same thing to me, many times. I don't want to have any regrets.

I want to be with one man and one man only, my husband, my true love. Now, it's not like I don't have hormones or like boys, I surely do. I know that most girls, maybe some girls, I really don't know enough to say most, can end up in the wrong place at the wrong time if they aren't cautious then nature just takes its course.

I don't want that ever to be me. Or Carol.

The kids have built a bonfire on the beach. The sun is going down behind us.

Carol tells me all about California, how neat it is to watch the sun set into the water, the reverse from here where we watch the sun rise out of the water. Not long after we arrive Rudy shows up with his buddy Clark in tow.

Clark likes me. Carol wants me to give him a chance, but there is no way that's going to happen. Clark has one thing on his mind, sex. He has been with a few girls, or so the rumor mill says. Like Rudy he is a football player, a halfback. I guess he's good enough to where Florida University has recruited him. That makes him a god in his mind, but it doesn't mean diddly squat to me.

"Hi Carol," Rudy says. "These are for you." Rudy hands Carol a bouquet of flowers. I know where he got 'em, at Silver's for a quarter.

"Hi Sonja," Clark says. "I'm glad you came."

"Hey," we say in return.

Carol has that look in her eye. Time for a story.

Before I can begin my story, Rudy breaks out the beer. I don't drink, or smoke, although almost everyone smokes, including

Carol. It always seemed like a filthy habit to me. My father reeks of tobacco and I associate the smell with him. That's enough right there for me never to touch a cigarette.

"Have a beer, Sonja," Clark urges.

"No thank you," I say, politely declining his invitation to loosen my inhibitions. "You're choice," Clark says, disappointed.

Carol drinks beer, but she knows to stop after one. "Did you guys hear about Nancy?"

"Which Nancy?" Rudy asks.

"Nancy Ridge," I answer. "She plays tenor saxophone in the band."

"What about her?" Rudy knows where I'm headed and he clearly does not want me to go there.

"She's pregnant. She had to drop out of school. You hadn't heard?"

"I heard something like that. Never can be sure if those stories are true."

"Oh, it's true. I don't know who the father is, though. Do you guys know?"

"Not a clue." Clark and Rudy are lying through their teeth. They know damn well that Reed Whipple is the father, their fellow ball player.

I had deliberately not shared this information with Carol, saving it for this moment. She didn't know Nancy as well as I did because Nancy went to my church.

Carol puts down her beer. My tale is having its desired effect.

"So, you guys up for a walk?" Rudy says, desperate to change the subject. "Sure," I say. "Let's go together. We can walk all the way to Ponte Vedra and hope that the snobs won't chase us away."

"I was thinking more about the ponds," Rudy responds.

I'll bet you were, I think. The ponds are famous for being the best necking place around. They're isolated and a hundred yards away from the beach or the road. I noticed that Rudy had brought along a basket with a blanket in it. Two blankets. My, my. That boy was always planning ahead.

"Let's go to Ponte Vedra, Rudy. Maybe we could sneak into the beach and sit at the tables since it'll be dark soon. We could pretend that we're all rich kids waiting for the hired help to prepare the yacht," Carol says.

Carol has caught on. I've done my good deed for the day. Not that I'm out to save the world or anything, I just love my friend and I want her to be able to go to California next year and not end up like poor Nancy, isolated and shunned – put away to avoid public embarrassment.

That was a fate to be avoided at all costs.

"Sonja, just a moment please."

"Yes, Mr. Porter?"

"How's the thumb?"

"Fully healed, thank you very much. I can play the cymbals again if you would like."

"I have something else in mind."

"Okay."

"How about the tenor saxophone?"

Nancy Ridge's spot. Of course, it had to be filled by someone.

"I played the sax for a bit last year in Augusta. It wouldn't take long to get up to speed."

"I'm sure you'll do fine. You are an excellent musician, young lady. The best I have in the band."

I blush. What a compliment. And he wasn't yelling. "Does this mean I can play in the pep band?"

"You are now a member of the pep band, Sonja. I know how much you wanted to be included."

"Thanks, Mr. Porter. I will make you proud."

"I spoke with your father yesterday."

Uh oh, I silently say.

"He is a…unique person."

"Mr. Porter, my father is a difficult man to deal with; you don't have to spare my feelings, I know."

"He was still concerned that somehow he owed the doctor money for your thumb. I explained to him weeks ago that it was covered through the school. He used the word 'charity' with me. He said that you were no one's 'charity case'. How could the school doing what it is required to do be considered charity?"

"Dad is very sensitive when it comes to money matters."

"So I see. Is everything all right at home, Sonja? I don't mean to pry, I'm just concerned."

"Yes, everything is fine. Thank you for asking."

"Just know that if you ever need to talk to someone I'm available, or I'll make sure that a female teacher is available."

I want to give him a hug and a kiss, but I think better of it. "Thanks, Mr. Porter. I really mean it."

The bell rings, fourth period is starting. Things are really looking up.

Maybe moving to Jacksonville was truly a blessing after all.

CHAPTER TEN

My life has a routine to it again, which gives me comfort. Seven days a week I'm fully occupied. Between my duties at home, school, band, my piano and the church music team I'm working hard, trying not to provide the devil any idle hands to work with. But that fiend is always working anyway, no matter what we do.

I'm busy putting things away and buttoning up the piano after the second Sunday service when Pastor Walker gets my attention.

"Sonja? Could I see you in my office please?"

When I walk into the pastor's office he is talking with Walter Barker. I sit in an empty chair and join the conversation.

"Sister Kent, I would like to ask for your assistance."

"Sure, Pastor. How can I help?"

"You know Sylvia Rogers, don't you?"

"Not very well. She's a Senior and she kind of keeps to herself. I know who she is, that's about it."

"Her brother, Tom, do you know him?"

"Nope. I didn't know that she had a brother."

"Well, 'had' is the right word, Sonja. Tom shot himself in the head last night, right in the family living room."

"Lord have mercy!" I shout.

"I knew Tom," Walter explains. "He was seeing Julie Reed until a couple of weeks ago. She took his engagement ring and then she dumped him. I warned him about her, but he was in love. It's a dang shame."

"I would like the two of you to pay a visit to the Rogers' home. I want Sylvia to know that her church supports her and cares. Be Christ to her."

"Certainly, Pastor," I say. "When would you like us to go?"

"Right now."

"My father expects me …"

"I stopped Jerry outside a few moments ago and told him that I needed you to visit someone for me. He knows that you won't be home until later."

I wish I had that kind of influence with my father.

"You two can take my car," the pastor says, handing Walter the keys. "You've been to the Rogers' house before, haven't you Walter?"

"Yes sir. I know how to get there."

"Great. Let's pray first and then off you go."

Walter and I have been working together at the church for a few months now, but we haven't really gotten to know each other very well. I think I intimidate him, or put him off some with my brashness. He is a very competent musician and a far better than average choir director. Like me, he is mature beyond his years and the adults recognize this and give him a great deal of responsibility.

More than a few times I've noticed him giving me the once over when he thought I wasn't looking. That's alright with me, I like Walter noticing me. I think he looks pretty good in his basketball uniform. As far as I know he's not dating anyone and I have heard nothing to suggest that Walter is a scamp or a drinker. I know that his parents own the biggest sporting goods store in town, Barker's, down on Main Street. They are one of the church's biggest financial supporters.

"When's the big game?" I ask knowing the answer, but I'm trying to make conversation.

"Thursday night. If we beat Daytona Beach, we make it to state."

"You guys will win, you beat 'em last time."

"We got lucky. If Roger hadn't hit those free throws…"

"And if you hadn't stolen the ball…"

Walter smiles. He likes being flattered. All boys do, especially about sports. "Well, I just hope we play well. I really want to go to Gainesville."

"Me too. Mr. Porter says that the pep band goes with the team this year if you guys make it to state."

"Sonja, have you ever done this before? Talked to someone about a suicide?"

"No. Have you?"

"No. Just remember to keep what's said to yourself. This is not a subject for school gossip."

"You don't know me very well, Walter. The last thing I am is a gossip."

"Things like this aren't talked about, ya know. That's all I'm saying." Walter is a little put off, or so I perceive.

"My lips are sealed. The only person I'll talk about this with is you."

"The police had to file a report of course, but the papers agreed not to run a story.

With any luck at all the whole thing will blow over in time."

"How does a boy shooting himself in the head 'blow over in time'?" I ask. "If people don't talk about it, it fades away."

"Keep up a good front and all that," I add.

"Yes, that's right. No need to embarrass anyone unduly."

Here we go, I think, but don't say. If us good Southern folks stick our heads in the sand and pretend somethin' doesn't exist, well then it just doesn't exist.

"Ready?" Walter asks. We have arrived. "As I'll ever be," I respond.

I like Walter. There is something about him that appeals. It doesn't hurt that he looks so dang good in those basketball shorts either.

"Good evening Mrs. Rogers," Walter says when she answers the door. "I'm Walter Barker and this is Sonja Kent. Reverend Walker sent us over to pay our respects and to talk with Sylvia."

Mrs. Rogers looks like a walking corpse. I've never seen a woman so shattered. When Aunt Mabel went through her hell she never looked this bad. My heart goes out to the poor woman.

With a nod and no words Mrs. Rogers let us in. The living room is torn up – someone has destroyed the furniture and smashed all the pictures. Shattered glass is lying atop pieces of broken lamps and tables. A huge blood stain is on the floor. It looks like someone has tried to clean it up, but they didn't quite succeed.

"Sylvia is in her room. Second door on the left," Mrs. Rogers says, looking neither of us in the eye. Walter can see that I desperately want to give the woman a hug and comfort her, but he motions that we should go and see Sylvia and leave Mrs. Rogers to her misery. I'm unsure what to do, so I follow Walter's lead.

"Hi, Sylvia," I say, feeling totally stupid. What am I supposed to say in this situation? I'm at a loss for words which for me is unprecedented.

"Oh my God," Sylvia moans as she collapses into my arms. She is shaking and crying so hard I worry that she might pass out. Walter looks at me and nods. Evidently I'm doing the right thing. We sit there for a while and let Sylvia do what she needs to do.

Walter prays. It's a nice prayer and, I believe, quite heartfelt. We say amen.

Sylvia will still not let me go.

Then Walter says, "We should pray for Julie. Her sin must be weighing heavily on her soul."

Sylvia seems to respond to Walter's idea and she lets me go and takes Walter's hand. Walter then asks the Good Lord to forgive Julie for driving Tom to kill himself. Evidently this is exactly what Sylvia needed to hear because she perks up a bit and thanks us for our visit. We have been in her room for over an hour.

As we leave we say goodbye to Mrs. Rogers who again cannot look us in the eye.

I'm considering all this as we are driving back to the church. I'm reflecting on the whole experience.

"You did a wonderful job, Sonja. The Lord is proud of you today."

"Do you know Julie Reed?" I ask.

"Not very well. Her father is a veterinarian, she works in his office. She's three years older than us."

"You said that you 'warned' Tom about her. What did you mean?"

"Julie is headstrong. I knew that she and Tom were fighting about things – where they were going to live, was she going to stop working after they were married and which church they were going to attend. You know, the stuff engaged people have to decide."

"You think it was her fault that Tom killed himself?"

"Only the Lord can decide that, Sonja. I do know that Julie dropped Tom like a hot rock when she couldn't get her way on certain things. That sent him over the edge."

"A real shame," I say.

I find myself feeling the worst for Julie, a girl I don't know. I can see where all this is headed.

Tom's suicide will be put in a box, wrapped with a bow and delivered right on Julie Reed's doorstep.

I don't know the particulars, but it seems real obvious to me that isn't just. The only one to blame for Tom killing himself was Tom.

CHAPTER ELEVEN

It's a dang shame, but it's true – I don't like spending time in my own home. I love my brothers and my mom and when we are all there without my father it can be real nice. But when he's around things go to hell quick. There is just no end to his misery.

Since we moved to Jacksonville his general temperament has gotten worse. I didn't think that was possible. At first I was encouraged by the fact that he seemed to have a renewed interest in God. He takes us to church every Sunday now, something he did not do in Augusta. But I can see that for what it is, he's just trying to impress Lord knows who. He wants people to think that he is an upstanding church going man and he got it in his head that this righteous perception will somehow magically wipe away the "stain" of being a debtor.

More than anything else I guess I feel sorry for him. He is trapped in this prison he has created for himself. The only thing he thinks about, night and day, is money.

What does this cost, how much does that cost, why did you have to buy that and on and on and on. I swear I don't know how, or why, my mother puts up with him.

Take today, for instance. Luke has had a toothache for a week now. He needs to see a dentist. You would think that a father would be concerned for his son's welfare and want to ease his suffering. Not my father. He yelled at Luke and told him that it was his fault his tooth hurt because he failed to "properly brush his teeth". He made him feel small again, worthless. I've learned to stand up for myself. I'm old enough to know that my father has some serious problems he needs to deal with and that I'm not responsible for them. He still makes me crazy enough to want to run out the door screaming, but I have my friends, my music, my life to escape to. Not poor Luke.

Dad laid all this on my mother, something else he always does. He yelled at her too and ordered her to find "a cheap damn dentist" to deal with Luke's problem. He demanded to know exactly what it would cost, down to the last penny, for Luke to have his tooth pulled before he would authorize Mom taking him to the dentist's office. I watched as she spent almost two hours on the phone calling around searching for the cheapest dentist in Jacksonville. After fifteen minutes it was obvious – pretty much all the dentists around here charge five dollars to pull a tooth. But eventually she found one fairly close by that would do it for four and a half.

She and Luke went off to get his tooth pulled. They were back in a couple of hours and my brother looked so relieved. Father didn't ask him if he was alright, how it went, nothing like that. All he could say was "I hope you learned your lesson. Take better care of your teeth from now on. Money don't grow on trees."

Lord have mercy if I hear that expression one more time before the day I die I swear I might just explode. "Money don't grow on trees." My father ought to go down to Nice's Music store and record that on vinyl and just play it over and over again for us all to hear throughout the day. I'm sick to death of his obsession with money.

Last Sunday Pastor Walker got me to thinking about my father in a new light. Sometimes the Gospel surprises me. Everyone knows the basics, but I think there is much more to it than the obvious.

Pastor was preaching a sermon on the evils of worshipping money. When he got to the part where the Good Book says, "The love of money is the root of all kinds of evil", I looked straight at my father. He was barely conscious, dozing off in his seat during the sermon, as usual. Anyway, the light bulb kind of switched on for me. My father doesn't love money in the way a greedy rich man does, he's not trying to hoard it or get more than his share. In a way his sickness is worse than that; he elevates money above everything else in life, he makes it his god. Idol worship, that's what my father is doing. I had never thought of it that way before, but it is so true. Everything he does is to please his god, stupid money. Combine that with his pride and, well, that's why I simply cannot stand to be around the man.

I'm trying my best to help Luke. He needs to build some self-esteem. I need to be relieved of some household duties. Seems like a perfect fit to me, but my father will not allow Luke to iron a shirt or fold the laundry. That is "women's work" to my father and no son of his is going to do "women's work". My mother thinks Luke is just too young to do chores like ironing. I've been ironing since I was ten, I remind her. My arguments fall on deaf ears, as usual.

Vince is easier to deal with because he's so small. He is one of those kids who does not need much tending to and that's nice. I don't get it, but my father has never said a harsh word to Vince. Now, give him time and I'm sure that will change, but come to think of it maybe I shouldn't say that. Maybe Vince will be spared his wrath and grow up thinking that his father is a good man. One can only hope, as Grandma Mary says.

As the summer moves on I find myself thinking more and more about my future.

In a year from now I can leave home. Emancipation seems like a far off dream, but it really isn't, it's right around the corner. A year ago I was sure that I would be headed to Converse College in Spartanburg in the fall of '57 to pursue a career in music. That dream is gone now. There is no way I can afford to go to Converse without a scholarship and when I left Augusta that door was closed to me forever.

I know that my father thinks that by arranging for me to play piano at the church he was somehow making up for my loss of Miss Bloom and Converse College. He knows better, but it's a lie he can tell himself to justify his actions. Since I started playing at the church he has more or less left me alone, which is a huge blessing.

Today I drifted back into my bad habit of feeling sorry for myself. This is wrong, and I know it. The best cure for a dose of the blues is Aunt Mabel. I called her this afternoon and we talked for an hour.

She is planning to visit us in the fall. Oh how that lifted my spirits! I do not know why, but whenever Aunt Mabel is around my father gets an incredible dose of act right. He is not only on his best behavior, he's a new man. Maybe someday someone will explain this to me, but I'm sure that the reason has to run deep. Mabel talks to me about just about everything, but not about that. All she will say about my father is that she "understands his ways".

Tomorrow I plan on going to the beach with Carol. We spend most of our free time together. She stopped seeing Rudy a few weeks back after she found out what he was all about. She got a summer job at the drive thru in Jacksonville Beach so she works four days a week, mostly at night.

I think it's time that I started dating some. Aunt Mabel agrees that I'm old enough now to where I should be "testing the waters", but the only boys I'm interested in are the college guys. Even though I'll be seventeen soon, I'm a little young to be dating those boys. Not that their pounding down my door or anything.

When school starts again in three weeks Carol and I have vowed to go on a few dates together. If I date a few boys maybe I'll figure out what I'm looking for in a husband.

The only thing I know for sure is that I'll never marry anyone like my father. I'd rather be dead.

CHAPTER TWELVE

"I think he's nice," Carol says.

"Well, I guess he's nice. But that hair! All the grease he puts on it. I'd be afraid to touch it," I say.

"I'll be sure to keep my cigarette away from his head too."

"Yea, if his head went up in flames, then where would we be!"

Carol and I are doing the "girls going to the restroom" thing which is, of course, a not so secret code for, "we want to take a walk and go talk about the boys in private". We're having a blast. The two boys we are with are okay, nothing serious. It's Saturday night at Neptune Beach and the biggest concern we have at the moment is whether or not our makeup is right.

"Miss us?" Carol asks as we re-join our dates by the fire. "Desperately," Carol's date, Jeff answers.

I like Jeff. He's tall, I like tall guys. He plays basketball. He's a Junior though and that might be a problem for me. Senior girls don't usually date Junior guys, but Carol doesn't seem to mind.

My date is Harry. He is Jeff's best friend, but I honestly can't see how they ever connected. Harry is anything but an athlete; I think he's trying hard to be a beatnik or something. Harry is as smart as a tack though and that makes up for a lot with me. More than anything else I like intelligent boys.

"We were talking about Johnny Cash," Harry says, picking right up where we left off.

I ask.

"I like him, but I'm more of a '*Guys and Dolls*' fan. Have you seen that movie?"

"Johnny speaks to me," Harry proudly proclaims.

"What in the world would Johnny Cash have to say to you?" Jeff jokingly mocks.

"His music is just so on edge. I dig it."

"You 'dig it'? What does that mean?" Carol asks.

"It means he likes it. That's Harry's new phrase. He heard that's what all the kids out in California are saying."

That got Carol's attention. "Have you been to California?" she asks. "No, but I'm goin' next year for sure."

"I lived in San Diego for four years."

Now Harry is fully engaged. "I can't wait to see San Diego. Tell me about it."

Jeff and I sit there for a half an hour while Carol and Harry talk California. It's like we just disappeared. I can see that Carol is interested in Harry, maybe more than just being friends.

Jeff winks at me; he can tell what's going on too.

"Hey Sonja, why don't you and I take a walk?" Jeff offers. "I'll buy you a milk shake. These two can talk California for a while. Perhaps us Southern folk should take our leave."

"Oh, we've been rude. Sorry, you guys," Carol apologizes.

"Nonsense," I say. "I'd love a shake, Jeff. Let's go. We'll be back in a while." No one is upset about switching dates; it happens all the time, no big deal.

I'm much more interested in Jeff, anyway.

"I've heard about you, you know. You're a legend down at Ozzies." I had never seen Jeff at Ozzies. "I like to play pinball."

"From what I hear you're the best pinball player in the city."

Why Jeff, you clever devil. Compliments will get you everywhere. "Do you hang out at Ozzies?"

"Not so much anymore. My mother's maiden name is Kearns."

Clearly this is supposed to mean something to me, but I don't get it. I look puzzled.

"Mr. Kearns, the man who owns Ozzies? He's my uncle. I worked there until about a year ago."

I smile. Small world.

"I hear that you're the star of the team this year." I return the flattery to see what happens next.

"I'm gonna give it my all, that's for sure. I'm aiming for a scholarship."

"Where do you want to go to school?"

"My first choice would the University of Georgia in Albany."

"Beautiful campus. I've been there twice."

Jeff buys me a chocolate shake from the stand. He's a nice boy. I am quickly starting to care less that he's not a Senior.

"Sonja, I don't want to make too much of it, but have you noticed that we're being watched?"

"No," I say, now a bit concerned. "Who is watching us?"

"Walter Barker. He's sitting right over there. He followed us up from the beach."

I glance in the general direction. "Walter. I know Walter rather well. He and I are part of the music team together down at the First Baptist Church."

"I don't think he likes me talking with you or buying you milk shakes."

"Don't be silly. Walter and I are just friends. We've never been on a date. It's not like that."

"I know the evil eye when it's sent my way. I'll bet he tells me tomorrow in gym to stay away from you."

"Well if he does tell him to mind his own business. I think I like you buying me milk shakes, Jeff."

I put my arm in Jeff's and we turn and walk away, back toward the beach.

"I can't believe this came out of my kitchen, made with my groceries. You put me to shame, Mabel."

"Faye, it's an easy recipe; a quick and dirty jambalaya. You can use any old kind of fish. The key is the sauce, that's what makes it."

"Yes, it's wonderful, Mabel. Thank you for cookin' for us. It's been a real treat," my father compliments.

Please God, I pray, let my father act like this when she's not around.

"I'll try and come down more often. I miss you all terribly. Augusta just hasn't been the same since you left."

"We miss you too. Maybe we can come and visit you soon," Faye says, looking at my father. He does not respond, he keeps his head down and continues eating.

"Sonja, are we still on for tonight?"

"Yes. Carol will be here in ten minutes."

"Great! I'm looking forward to seeing your favorite haunts."

"Goin' somewhere, Sonja?" Now my father takes an interest in the conversation. "Yes. Carol and I are going to show Mabel our school, Ozzies and maybe drive down to the beach."

"Carol's drivin'?"

"Yes."

"Well maybe we …"

"That's alright with you, isn't it Jerry? I don't want to cause problems."

"Sure, that's fine. Ya'll go have a good time."

Unbelievable.

If I could only do what Aunt Mabel can do this home wouldn't be such a bad place to live.

CHAPTER THIRTEEN

My illness came upon me suddenly. Carol and I were sitting in the back of civics class late one afternoon paying not so close attention to Mr. Rader. Listening to him lecture on American government was about as thrilling as watching paint dry. As Mr. Monotone was droning on, I began to feel peculiar. When it started it felt like cramps. My cycle had just ended, so I knew it wasn't menstruation. The cramps moved from my belly to my arms and legs. I tried to squirm and wiggle and loosen myself up, but that only made it worse.

Then my head began swimming. I felt dizzy and almost threw up all over the desk. Thank the Good Lord that Carol was sitting right beside me, she noticed that I was in distress. She tried, I think, to get my attention a couple of times, but I really don't remember everything that happened. The next thing I knew two big football players were carrying me off to the nurse's office.

When I woke up, I suppose "came around" is a more accurate description because I never really passed out, the nurse was holding my hand and taking my blood pressure. She gave me some apple juice and as I sipped it I felt better. The cramps were gone, but I was sore, like someone beat me up or something.

"What happened to me?" I ask the nurse.

"I'm not sure. Could just be a dizzy spell, but you were all knotted up so it might be somethin' else. You ma's comin' to get ya. She's gonna take you to the doc and get you checked out."

By the time my mother arrives it is nearly four o'clock, an hour after the school day ended. She smiles at me and asks if I can walk. I can walk, but it's difficult. Every muscle in my body aches. I'm scared. I worry that I might have polio or some other horrible disease that will cripple me for life.

"Your father called the chiropractor," Mom explains. "They're waitin' for us right now."

"Who?"

"Your father and the chiropractor."

"Wonderful." The last thing, the *very* last thing, I need right now is to be around my father.

I have been to the chiropractor's office once before for the treatment of the flu, of all things. My father believes that a chiropractor can cure all. It doesn't matter what's wrong – cold, broken bone, headache, anything – his answer is to take us to see the chiropractor. My father's faith in this "miracle worker" is no doubt bolstered by the fact that he is dirt cheap. Doctor's cost real money, chiropractic treatments are inexpensive.

That he gets exactly what he pays for is not a consideration to my father. If the "adjustment" doesn't have the desired effect, that's our fault, I guess.

So I sit there, sore as all creation, and let this fool spine bender twist me like a pretzel. It hurts like crazy, but I try not to complain. Maybe there is something to this mumbo-jumbo after all, I try to convince myself.

An hour later, when he's done, I feel worse. But I say "thank you" and leave with my parents. Once home I collapse in my bed. Kraus crawls in with me and, at last, I have some peace.

After I got sick at school I stayed home for a few days, but I haven't really felt the same since. I've become best friends with the aspirin bottle. Now it's nearly May and I'm trying my best to deal with this malaise as I look forward to graduation.

My father thinks that I've become lazy. I just don't have the energy anymore to cook and clean and do everything else he and mom expect me to do. So he yells and carries on and threatens to take away my piano time at the church and make me stop playing in the band unless I "get with it" around the house. I can't wait to leave home, but I need to feel better before I can take the next step.

Mother did have some encouraging news today. She told me that in thirty days her health insurance from the Navy Yard kicks in and then she can take me to see a doctor for free. I'm not sure that a doctor can help me, but I desperately want to try. It's hard to live life not feeling well and I'm too young to be suffering from something like this, that's for sure.

"Sonja, Walter is here," Luke calls out. "Tell him I'll be right there," I answer.

Ever since that day at Neptune Beach a few months back, Walter Becker has not been shy about expressing his affections toward me. We've gone out on a few group dates and we spend hours each week at the church together. I'm not sure how I feel about him yet, but there are several things that appeal.

He comes from a prominent family. His father and mother are regular church goers and they seem like nice people, but I notice that Walter's mother coddles him. Walter is an only child. I suppose that all only children are spoiled to some degree.

Of course, it doesn't hurt that Walter looks nice in his basketball shorts. "Sonja!" my father yells. "Are you goin' out?"

"Yes sir."

"With Walter?"

"Yes sir."

"And who else?"

"No one else, just he and I. We're going to the movies, to see '*Around The World in Eighty Days*.'"

My father says not another word; he's heading for the door. No doubt Walter is about to get an ear full. I grab my purse and follow behind at a safe distance.

"Walter," my father says, opening the door. "Mr. Kent, good evening sir."

"Whose car ya drivin?"

"My father's car, sir."

"Nice machine. What's that, a new Chevy?"

"Yes sir, we just bought it last winter."

"I don't want my daughter to see the back seat of that fancy car, am I makin' myself clear, Walter?"

"Yes sir. I treat Sonja with respect, sir. At all times."

I liked hearing that and it was true, Walter does treat me with respect. "See to it, young man. Sonja will be home by ten. Not a moment after."

"We will not be late sir. We are going to the drive thru and to the movies and back here, nowhere else."

"Just because you have some money in your pocket doesn't make you *special* boy, you understand?"

"Let's go, Walter," I say as I walk past my father and out the door. "We'll be late if we don't get moving."

"Thanks, Sonja," Walter says as he opens the car door for me. "Your father is a hand full."

"Tell me about it."

CHAPTER FOURTEEN

"What is it?" I ask mother, who is carefully examining the small lump on my neck."

"Can't be sure, but it has to be related to your weakness spells. It only makes sense."

"Carol's father says he thinks it might be a goiter. What's a goiter?"

"Comes from having a bad thyroid, that's all I know."

"When can we go see the doctor?"

"Next week, Sonja. I've already made the appointment."

"Thank God."

"Let me tell your father."

"Why? I thought it was free for us now."

"It is, but convincing him of that... let me tell him."

"Okay." I just want the thing looked at and removed. Now I have a lump in my neck? And right before the Senior Prom? Thank goodness it isn't too noticeable yet.

I was forced to endure two more sessions with the chiropractor. Each time I just got angrier. What a waste of money. Now, I've not been to medical school, but what dope would think that adjusting your spine could get rid of a lump in your neck? Other than my father no one was that stupid. I'm sure that the chiropractor has a good laugh every time he goes to the bank to deposit his money. He must believe that everyone who comes to see him is a complete idiot.

Mother put an end to my chiropractor visits. I'm not sure how she got my father to relent, but she did.

"Are you ready to open the box?" Mother asks.

"I've been ready since yesterday when it got here," I answer. "I'm kinda excited too, honey. Did she tell you much about it?"

"Only that it was light blue. Aunt Mabel wanted the style to be a surprise."

My mother wants to be part of my Senior Prom. She is taking an interest in me lately, much more so than usual. I think she realizes that sooner rather than later I'll be gone and she knows that I will not be coming back.

We open the box together and pull out the prom dress. It has been carefully wrapped in sheer fabric to keep it from wrinkling.

It is a gorgeous formal evening dress with a very low cut back. I can tell that I will be squeezing into it because it is also very form fitting. Two long, white evening gloves are included in the package.

"Sonja," mother says, amazed. "Mabel sure out did herself this time. Can't imagine anything prettier."

I envision what it will be like to walk into the prom with my dress on, my hair done up, makeup perfect and a pair of high heels on my feet. I'll look just like a Hollywood actress.

"I love Aunt Mabel," I say with tears in my eyes. "What is Walter wearing?"

"A black tux, I'm sure. Don't all the boys wear tuxedoes?"

"You might need an armed escort to keep Walter off of you, dear."

"He knows to behave himself. We've had that conversation."

"What conversation was that?"

"That I'm not the type of girl who puts out."

"Good for you. All things in due time."

"Mom," I ask, knowing that I'll get no real answer, "what's it like? Sex, I mean? Is it fun?"

There are two things in this world that my mother never likes to talk about, my father and sex. I suppose both are closely connected.

"It's like blinking your eyelids. You don't have to think about it, the whole thing is natural."

Like blinking your eyelids? What does that mean? I say in my head.

"Do you like it?"

"Men like it, Sonja. Women too, I guess, but it's much more important to men."

"So it's not fun?"

"It's different for everyone. Why are you asking me about this right now? Is Walter after you to have sex with him?"

"He would if I'd let him, that's for sure. I guess that makes him a typical boy, huh."

"Pretty much."

"I think he's going to ask me to marry him."

Mother sets down the dress and turns and looks at me intently. "Why do you say that?"

"He's been hinting around about it for a couple of weeks, making sure that I know that he has a great job at the store waiting for him after school, that his father plans on giving him the store when he retires, how much he wants kids, you know, all the signs."

"What would you say if he asks?"

"I'm leaning toward yes."

"I like Walter. I think he would make a good husband, Sonja."

"Does Dad like him?"

"I think he's warmed to him a bit, as much as would warm to any boy after his daughter."

"Well he hasn't asked me yet, but he is thinking about it, no doubt."

"Are you really going?"

"Harry and I are leaving on June tenth. I'm going to stay with my Dad's friends in San Diego and Harry says that he has enough money saved to rent an apartment."

"Where did Harry get any money?"

"His grandmother passed last fall and left him some."

"Are you in love with him, Carol?" I ask.

"I don't know. I really like him. We'll see what happens when we get out to California."

"Tell him to wash his hair."

"I know! That's the worst part. He has to change that greasy hair do!"

"You don't seem to mind."

"He makes up for it in other ways."

"He does?"

"You know, he's very affectionate."

"You two…I mean…"

"Yes, a few times now. Don't worry. We use protection. Your lectures haven't fallen on completely deaf ears."

"You don't, I mean you didn't want to wait for …'

"Sonja, honey. I lost my virginity when I was fifteen. Remember, I grew up around sailors. They're the worst."

"You never told me." I'm a little disappointed in Carol. Not so much for her loose morals as for her keeping such a secret from me.

"You mean you and Walter…you haven't?"

"No," I reply sternly. I suddenly feel a distance between us and I don't like it. I really don't like the idea that very soon she'll leave and I'll never see her again. "You're mad at me, aren't you? I'm sorry, Sonja. I should have told you about Harry. It's not like I sleep around. He's the only boy I've been with in Jacksonville."

I'm not sure why, but I am mad at Carol. She talks about sex so casually, like it's no big deal. Well, it's a big deal to me. I guess I want a friend like me, someone who believes everything just like I do. Maybe it's this damn malaise I'm suffering through.

All I know for sure is that I'm losing my best friend. What will I do without her?

CHAPTER FIFTEEN

I finally know what's wrong with me. Carol's dad was right; this lump on my neck is a goiter. The doctor says I have hyperthyroid syndrome, meaning that a little gland pumps out too much of whatever it's supposed to pump out. He gave me some medicine to take, an iodine solution of some kind. He said it would probably ease the symptoms some until he can operate and take part of the gland out of my neck. That, he believes, will solve the problem.

I do feel better, and none too soon. My lump was never very noticeable, and it has retreated some after only a few days of taking the solution. You have to touch it to know it's there. Thank you, Jesus. I have on this beautiful dress, I'm ready to go to the prom and my worst nightmare is not coming true, I won't look like a gargoyle with an orange stuck in my throat after all.

Kraus doesn't know what to think of his mamma in this gorgeous blue dress.

He's looking at me like I'm an alien from Mars or something. But I can't pet him. No dog hair or any other foreign object is going to mar this perfection.

"Sonja," mom says as she walks into the bathroom and sees me admiring myself. "You're all grown up." She starts to cry.

"Don't you dare," I lovingly chide her. "If you get me going, I'll ruin my makeup."

"I wish your father could see you."

"He can look at the pictures if he wants." The best thing about my day so far is that my father has been working at his part time job at the ship yard so he hasn't been around to say something horrible.

"Tell me all about it again."

"Mom, I've already told you…" I stop when I look into her eyes. She is enjoying my prom experience as much, or maybe even more, than I am. "Okay. Walter and Harry and Tim, Walter's other basketball buddy, are coming to get me at six. Then we pick up Carol and Tim's date, I don't know her yet. We are going out to dinner at Jimmy's, the restaurant on the beach…"

"The one where it costs fifty bucks just to sit down…"

"Yea, that one. Then we are going to the prom. I'm not sure when the prom ends."

"You get home whenever it suits you, honey. I told your father that this is your special night. He never went to his prom. He doesn't care for such things, I suppose, but I understand, honey."

"I think he's going to ask me tonight."

"More signs?"

"A bunch. He's more nervous than a long tailed cat in a room full of rocking chairs."

We laugh. That is Grandpa Lester's favorite saying. "What will you tell him if he asks?"

"Yes. I'll say yes."

"Are you sure?"

"How can you know for sure?"

"You can't. Things just happen the way they happen, I suppose."

I have to ask her. I think a daughter has the right to ask her mother this question when she is considering marriage.

"Are you glad that you married Daddy?"

"Sonja, why would you…" Mom turns and starts to walk away. I thought she was going to leave me standing there in the bathroom looking like Cinderella waiting for her carriage without giving me an answer.

But she stops by the bathroom door, turns around and says, "When I look at you and your brothers I'm not sorry that I married your father. Not one bit."

"What looks good to you, Sonja?"

"It all looks good, Walter. Why don't you order for me?" I know exactly what I'd like to order, but I want Walter to feel special and in charge more than I want lobster.

"We'll both have the lobster," Walter says speaking with confidence, like he visits fancy restaurants all the time.

"I love the white sport coat and the pink carnation," I say. "I assumed you'd wear a black tux, but this was a much better choice." I adjust Walter's collar and brush a stray thread off of his jacket.

"I wanted to look my best for you, Sonja. Tonight is our night."

A jazz trio playing in the restaurant strikes up a tune just as Walter is expressing his affections.

Carol leans over and whispers in my ear, "Well, is he going to ask you?"

"Lord, I hope not here in front of everyone. He wouldn't do that, would he?"

"There is no telling what he might do."

"We need to go to the ladies room."

"Let's go."

When we announce our departure, all the boys stand. Such deference and respect, I wish it was prom night every night.

"Harry seems all relaxed and sure of himself, as usual."

"He's growing on me. He's a really good guy when you get past the shell."

"Maybe you two will get married."

"Not a chance, Sonja. I'm not getting married for a while."

"What about Harry, what if he asks you?"

"He won't. We've talked about it. He wants to explore the world, I think. But we are good together for now."

Carol and I are so different. I reached the conclusion since her "revelation" to me that I have no right to judge other people, especially someone as dear to my heart as Carol. Just because she doesn't believe the way I believe about certain subjects does not mean that she is any less of a friend.

"Do you need this? I thought you might." Carol hands me a condom.

"Lord, put that away!" I exclaim. I look around in a mad panic hoping to heaven that no one else in the ladies room saw Carol pull that thing out of her purse.

"It's only a condom, Sonja. I know that you know what it's for."

"I do not need a condom. Gracious no." Just the sight of that little blue package makes my stomach turn.

"What if Walter asks you to marry him? If you say yes, then, well, he might expect you to ...?"

"If that's what he expects then he can find another girl," I declare with conviction. "I'm saving myself for my wedding night."

"Good for you, honey," Carol says, sincerely I think. "You are a woman with her own mind, Sonja. That's why I love you so much. I wish you were coming to California with me, we could have some great times together out there."

Until this moment the possibility of leaving everything and everyone behind and driving to California with Carol has never seriously crossed my mind. I take a second to contemplate the possibility.

"I'd really like to visit you, but my life is here," I say. "I'm a creature of the South, I'm afraid."

She kisses me on the cheek and we return to the table. Lord I'm going to miss my friend.

"I think Greg and Rhonda are the perfect Queen and King," I say to Walter, after our third slow dance.

"I agree, I guess. Sonja?"

"Yes, Walter?"

"Would you like another glass of punch?"

"Sure, that would be nice."

It's past eleven now and some of the kids have started to leave. Harry and Carol are headed out the door to go do – well, I'm not going to say what they are going to go do. They said that they were calling a cab. Tim and his date, Ilene, have already left, I don't know with whom.

I'm certain that Walter has set all this up. He will be driving me home, alone. "Sonja," Walter says with a glass of punch in his hand, "after you finish this, can we leave? I'd like to show you something."

"Sure." Am I building this up in my mind? Maybe all Walter wants to do is to try and have sex with me. If that's what he is planning then he is about to be greatly disappointed, I promise myself.

I take one long last look around at my Senior Prom. The room is decorated in red and white, our school colors. The band is playing Pat Boone's *"Love Letters in the Sand"*. For the first time since I was forced to move to Jacksonville, everything seems right. So far it has been a perfect night—a nice young man from a good family is pursuing me and at least I know what the heck is wrong with my neck and I can fix it.

How often do you get a moment like this in your life? For me everything good is now possible and soon, one way or another, I will be free from the tyranny of my father.

Walter is very anxious. It's time to go. High school is now a thing of the past.

CHAPTER SIXTEEN

"Where are we going?"

"I want to show you something. It's about ten minutes from here. I'd like it to be a surprise."

"Okay."

Walter has my heart fluttering, in a good way. I have no idea where he is taking me, but I'm not uncomfortable, just the opposite. It feels right and natural sitting in the car next to Walter Barker driving around town. He is treating me the way I want to be treated, like somebody special, someone worthy of love and respect.

I swear that I can hear bells, but maybe that's just my imagination, or the radio.

Anyway, I'm lost in a dreamy fog.

"There it is," Walter says, pointing across a lawn at a nice little house. "There what is?" I ask.

"Our new home. A friend of my father's owns the place and, well, I told him that I was hoping to be starting a family." Walter reaches into his pocket and pulls out a small black box. He gently takes my hand. He opens the box, hands me the ring and asks, "Will you marry me?"

I hear the bells again, but I ignore them. "Yes Walter, I will marry you."

"I love you, Sonja."

"I love you, Walter."

We kiss. We had kissed before of course, but not like this. Walter is very passionate. I allow him to French kiss me, something I had never done before. He likes that and he moves his hand over my breast. I allow that too. His touch is gentle and I like it.

"Should we wait?" Walter asks. "Wait for what?"

"You know Sonja, to be together. To have sex."

"Walter, yes we should wait." I'm hearing Carol's voice in my head, explaining to me that all boys want sex. Walter clearly wants me, not just sex. I do not want to react to his advances like I am repelled by him, just chaste.

"I will wait for you, Sonja."

"You are going to be my husband. The only man I will ever be with for the rest of my life."

Walter clearly likes this idea. We kiss again and grope a little. We make out in his car for the better part of an hour.

"Let's go inside," Walter says. "You have the key?"

"Of course, like I said the house is ours. It will sit vacant until we move in."

"It's really nice."

"I'd say. It's a full karat, at least."

I blush. I know nothing about diamonds, but I do know that I love my ring. "Did you, you know?"

"No, Carol. He wanted to, but I told him that I wanted to wait until our wedding day."

"How many bases did you pass?"

"Bases?"

"You know, first base, second base, th…"

"I'm not sure what all the bases stand for," I say, laughing, "but we rounded second, I'll bet."

"You are my best friend in the whole world, have I told you that lately?"

Oh Lord, I knew she was going to say something like that. Now I'll start to cry.

Again.

"Do you have to go?" I sound like a child begging her mother not to leave her at home with the sitter.

"Honey, I can't stay here. If you'd come to California, you'd see why I like it so much. The weather is perfect. Seventy in the day, sixty something at night. Every day, year round. The beaches, the boys…"

"What about Harry?" I ask, interrupting. "What about him?"

"Aren't you guys together, a couple, I mean?"

"Yea, for now. He isn't Mr. Forever, sweetie."

"What do you want to do, when you get to California, I mean?"

"I've thought about going into nursing."

Now I laugh. A big, full roar of a laugh. "What's so funny?" Carol asks.

I can tell she is a bit hurt by my laughter. "Honey, you dropped like a stone looking at my torn up thumb. Remember that?"

"I do. That whole incident got me thinking. I kind of liked everything up to that point – helping you, watching the hospital people work, all of it. I've been sort of practicing since then."

"Practicing?"

"I got in touch with one of the nurses that I met that night. She said that I should volunteer as a 'Candy Striper', a sort of nurse's aide. I've been doing it for two weeks now. Believe it or not, I don't faint at the sight of blood anymore."

"So that's where you've been. I thought you were with Harry or maybe working some extra hours at the drive thru."

"I didn't want to tell you because I was sure you'd laugh at me."

Now I feel horrible. "I'm so sorry. I think you'll make a great nurse."

"Really?"

"Really."

"Some of the doctors are to die for too."

I recall my own flash of a crush on the doctor who fixed my thumb. "Maybe you'll end up marrying one. Doctor and Mrs. Carol."

"Sonja, I want to ask you something. I'm not trying to say that you're making a mistake by marrying Walter. It's just that I love you very much and…"

"Go ahead, honey," I say, gently touching her hand.

"You are a great pianist. I mean it, Sonja. I don't think you know how good you really are. Don't you want to give that a try? You could apply for scholarships; maybe get a student loan or something. If you get married and start a family you may never get a chance to pursue that dream."

"Walter says that he will buy me a piano. I plan on playing more, maybe finding a new teacher. I've thought about it, but right now I want out of my father's house and into my own home. I know my life sounds pretty dang boring to you, but …"

"No, honey," Carol says. "I didn't mean it that way at all. You are a really special person Sonja—smart as a whip, gorgeous and talented. Sometimes I worry that you haven't seen enough of the world, that you are selling yourself short."

"Don't you like Walter?"

"I do, but…"

"Don't hold back; say what's on your mind."

"Once you're married you'll find out who he is really is, honey. There is no way to tell for sure until then."

"I know who Walter is, what makes him tick. I mean I've been with him at the church for almost a year, we've been dating since…"

Carol reaches over and gives me a kiss on the cheek and a strong hug. "For someone so smart, you are so innocent. Men say whatever they have to say to get what they want and Walter definitely wants you. That's good, for sure. But you don't know him yet, Sonja. I hope and pray he is as advertised."

"You worry too much, Carol. Walter loves me. He will be a great husband."

"He better be, or I'll march right back here and straighten him out."

I have so much on my mind. Tomorrow two things are happening that I've been dreading for weeks. Carol and Harry are leaving for California and I'll be checking into the hospital for surgery on my thyroid. A true double whammy.

Right now though I just want to sit here on the boardwalk with my best friend and enjoy our evening together. I hate goodbyes. I hope that we are not saying goodbye forever.

But that's the thing about the future. It's uncertain.

CHAPTER SEVENTEEN

I'm tired of people pestering me, constantly asking me the same question, how do I feel? I know they mean well and I try to be polite, but for heaven's sakes! The doctor is going to slice open my throat and remove part of my thyroid. That's not the type of thing anyone wants to go through, but I know that I need the operation.

Walter is definitely passing his first test as a husband to be. He has been there for me not only today, but whenever I've needed him. My father is nowhere to be seen and that's not a complaint. Even with the best of intentions, which I'm not sure he ever has, he really just doesn't care. He certainly did care about what all this would cost. It took mother more than a few conversations to convince him that her insurance would pick up the entire tab for my care. Once Dad accepted that as truth, he lost interest in the whole subject of me going under the knife.

Lord in heaven I'll be glad when Walter and I are married and can see my father only on occasion and on my terms. God grant me that, I pray.

Grandma Mary has come to down to be with me. What a blessing! I wish Mabel was here, but I know she's tied up right now with matters in Augusta. Mother has been very attentive.

"Ready, Miss Kent?" the nurse asks.

I think about Carol and wonder if someday soon she'll be asking people the same question. "As I'll ever be," I respond.

Walter kisses me; Mom and Grandma squeeze my hand. Off I go.

"Miss Kent? Miss Kent?"

When I open my eyes the first feeling I have is nausea. I was told to expect this and they weren't kidding. I'm glad that there isn't much on my stomach because it wouldn't be there for long; I'd be looking at it all over my robe.

"Miss Kent?"

"Yes, present." Why I answer like a student in class I don't know.

"You'll feel groggy for a while. That's normal. Everything went very well, dear.

Please don't try and move your head."

As I wake up, I realize that my head is stuck between two sandbags; wedged in tighter than a drum is a more accurate description.

"How long do I have to stay like this?" They probably told me this before, but right now I'm not sure of much.

"Four days. Then you can go home."

"Four days. I can't..." I have to stop talking because whatever food I had in me is now coming out. Grandma Mary holds the bedpan under my chin so I don't make a mess all over my bed.

"This is a lot of fun," I say, as I take a sip of water.

"C'mon child. You hafta bear with it now. I'm here. Grandma will take care of ya."

I say something like "Thanks" or "God bless" or whatever. Then I pass out.

"I'm feeling sorry for myself. It's not very pretty."

"Hospital stays make us cranky, angel. I've been through a couple. It'll pass." Aunt Mabel knows just what to say to me.

"Not soon enough."

"Let's talk about something else."

"Let's, I'd love to."

"Is your mother coming back today?"

"Yep, she'll be here in a few minutes. She's bringing Luke with her."

"You can go home tomorrow?"

"That's what they say. No complications so far."

"See? It's almost over. Let's focus on your wedding."

I have to shift positions. I am so tired of this damn bed and head restraint. Just the simple act of talking on the phone is a major chore. Grandma Mary moves the earpiece to the other side.

"I have my ring back on. Sometimes I just sit and look at it. I like the way the diamond sparkles in the light."

"How is Walter? Is he still 'sparkling'?"

"I don't know why he puts up with me. I've been a real pain in the derriere for the past week. He's probably reconsidering his options about now."

"I doubt that, angel. That boy is head over heels in love with you."

"He's working full time at the store now and I think he likes it. When you come down I'll take you to see the place. It's huge, Mabel."

"Are you going to work there?"

"Heavens no. Me work? Walter wouldn't stand for that."

"What do you want to do?"

"To get the hell out of here, that'd be a great start."

"I'm serious."

"Play the piano, raise kids, be a good wife. What else is there?"

"The world is a great big place. You don't know that yet. That's my biggest worry for you, Sonja. You seem determined to become a married adult awfully fast."

"Do you regret marrying Uncle Porter and not seeing the world?"

"My situation was a bit different than yours. And you know that I love Porter with all my heart and soul. I still miss him every day."

I know how much Mabel loves my uncle. I just wanted to hear her express her devotion to him because I want to feel the same way ten years from now about Walter.

"Not having to live with my father will be like being released from prison." Mabel laughs. She often uses humor to diffuse my anger towards my father. "Jerry isn't that bad, angel."

"You try living with him."

"No thanks," Mabel says, chuckling. "Has he been around to see you?"

"Once. He asked how I was doing, but before I could answer him he said, 'Take care, gotta go' and he took off headed for another part time job. I think he's handed me off to Walter in his mind. That's a good thing, believe me."

"Your pattern arrived today."

"It did!" This is great news. Aunt Mabel sent all the way to Austria for the pattern to make my wedding dress.

"I'll start cutting the fabric for it next week. I promise you that no other bride in Florida will have a dress like yours, Sonja. I consider this dress to be my masterpiece."

"What would I ever do without you?" It is not a rhetorical question. I would surely be lost without Mabel, especially now that Carol is gone.

"Love you, child."

Mom and Luke come in and Grandma Mary hands the phone to my mother. She and Mabel talk for a minute and then she hangs up.

"Those are beautiful, Mom. Thanks. I need some cheering up."

"I got 'em from that florist down by Ozzies. The one next to that great colored restaurant, you know, the rib place."

Luke tells me jokes. He's been very taken lately with "knock-knock" jokes. A few of them are even funny.

"Okay, sis. I gotta another one."

"Let's hear it."

"Knock, knock!"

"Who's there?"

"Banana."

"Banana who?"

"Knock, knock!"

"Who's there?"

"Banana."

"Banana who?"

"Knock, knock!"

"Who's there?"

"Banana."

"Banana who?"

"Knock, knock!"

"Who's there?"

"Orange."

"Orange who?"

"Orange you glad I didn't say 'banana' again?"

I laugh. Luke can always do that for me; make me smile when I'm down.

What will life be like for him when I am gone? I worry that Dad will direct all of his venom toward Luke once I become Mrs. Barker.

But what can I do? Pray, that's about it.

CHAPTER EIGHTEEN

I didn't even get the chance to say goodbye.

Since I'll be leaving soon, Dad asked Luke if he would be willing to take care of Kraus. I wish I could take Kraus with me to my new home, but that's not possible. Luke has never been close to my dog; he doesn't really have a strong desire for any type of pet. Anyway, I guess Luke gave Father the answer he didn't want to hear some time back. He has been looking for a good home for Kraus ever since, or so I learned today.

When I got home from work I called for Kraus and he didn't come. I knew that something was wrong because he always comes when I call, without exception. When I noticed that his bowls and dog house were missing, it wasn't hard to figure out that Kraus was now a memory.

Of course my Father didn't bother to say a word to me about it. He let Mom break the bad news. "He went to a good home, honey," was all she said. She wouldn't tell me who or where – I guess they were afraid I'd go retrieve him if I knew where he was.

A year ago something like this would have devastated me. But now I have bigger fish to fry. I will take it on faith that Kraus is with a nice family and happy and not missing me too much. Soon

I'll have to get used to sleeping with a man, not a dog. Perhaps losing Kraus is for the best.

I called Mabel and cried to her a bit about Kraus, but that was not the main topic of our conversation. She is steamed, I mean really mad, about me having to go to work to pay for my own wedding. A month ago, when all this was decided, I passed by the living room and I could hear her yelling at my mother through the phone. I've never heard her so angry.

As for me, I took it in stride. The Barkers have plenty of money. They would be happy to pay for the whole affair, but my father would not accept their generosity. This should have surprised no one. If the man can't bring himself to let a court of law settle his debts like everyone else does, why should anyone have expected him to allow the groom's parents to pay for the bride's share of the wedding?

Since he was not going to pay for it but neither would he allow the Barker's to do so, it fell on me to get a job and cover the bill. Of course, my father will present the check to the Barkers and take the credit for holding up his end of the expenses. I'm not sure if I'm going to tell Walter about the whole thing until after we are married. Until we tie the knot I still live under my father's roof and Walter knows it is not his place to question if I work or not, or where or what I do with my money.

I like my job. It's nice to be out in the world and not stuck in the house all day or sitting in a classroom. I work at Barnett Bank as a receptionist. I greet people as they come in, answer the phone, deliver messages and help out at various tasks. I have to look nice every day, which pleases me.

Once I'm officially Mrs. Barker I'm almost positive that my working career will be over, at least for a while. Walter does not want a working wife. In fact I think he considers the very idea a touch scandalous. I'm marrying into a very traditional family, which I like. They have a certain position in Jacksonville. They belong to the Yacht Club. Even though their boat is nice, I don't think it's a yacht, but that's beside the point. They run in certain social circles, support causes and charities and regularly host dinners and parties. I like the idea of becoming part of their group.

What I'm not too fond of is an August wedding. Why August? Mrs. Barker, who I can see is very much the Queen Bee when it comes to family matters, insisted on the date. It does give me enough time, *just*, to pay my family's share of the bill. For that reason mainly, and there were others, I didn't argue about the timing.

There certainly is no question about where the ceremony will be held, at our church. The entire congregation will be invited, along with a long list of guests that are mostly relatives and friends of the Barkers. That's what I have all spread out in front of me right now, the wedding invitations. I've come to realize what a big deal this whole wedding invitation thing is. I never knew. Some people only get invited to the reception, not the wedding. Folks are expected to RSVP at least three weeks prior to the nuptials. I guess that's because they need to know how much food to provide and where everyone's going to sit.

One thing we have to do is hire someone to play music for us. Walter and I can't be expected to play at our own wedding! This is a labor of love for me. I know just what music I want and how I want it played. Mrs. Barker doesn't put her hands into this aspect of our big day; it's all up to me.

The reception will be at the Yacht Club. From the looks of it there will be over two hundred people attending, maybe thirty or forty of whom are from my family or are my friends.

I really want Carol to come back for the wedding and be my maid of honor, but I know that's not possible. Walter told me that he would have his father pay for her ticket to come out, bless his heart. Carol is enrolled in school. There is no way she can just up and leave for a week to be here for me. She applied to college as soon as she got to San Diego and now she is taking a full course load in whatever someone studies to become a nurse. I'm so happy for her.

Carol and Harry broke up less than a month after they got to San Diego. Carol says they parted friends and that he even calls her and they talk like pals now. I don't get that, I really don't. How do you go from being lovers to being friends? Just like that?

I suppose love is different for everyone. I can tell that Walter is chomping at the bit to have sex with me. Last week, during one of our heavy petting sessions, he put my hand on his crotch. I had never touched a man's private parts before. I have to admit I was curious so I let me hand stay there for a second or two. Boy did I learn my lesson.

You'd have thought Walter had been shot out of a cannon. He had my shirt off, down to the bra, before I could catch my breath. He was reaching around to unclasp my brassiere and then do Lord knows what when I had to shove him off of me. He didn't like that one bit. He came at me again and I had to get up and take a few steps back as I put my shirt on.

He had this look in his eye. He was very determined. I was something he wanted and he wanted it right now. It scared me a little. After a minute or two, when he could see that it was not going any further, he backed off, but he was angry and disappointed. He pouted for the rest of the day.

I talked to Carol and Mabel about what happened. I guess Walter is just a normal guy. Me, when I think of sex I think about tenderness and cuddling and soft kisses. What comes to mind are things like candles and pretty nighties. Sex is supposed to be a bond, the glue that keeps a couple close. Mabel told me that she and Porter would sometimes stay in bed all day wrapped in each other's arms. That's what I want, the closeness.

Men are not the same and I better learn that real quick, Carol told me. Men want to do it, be done with it, recover and do it again. For them it's physical first, emotional second, Carol explained. For most women it's the reverse. It certainly is for me.

But I'm sure that every bride has to struggle with these issues. I don't think Walter is different than any other man. We'll figure it out together.

It will probably be a whole lot easier than dealing with all of these stupid invitations.

CHAPTER NINETEEN

It seems more like a movie than something real to me. Our little church house is packed, standing room only. The weather has cooperated too; it's a lovely day, sunny and eighty five degrees. The outside walls of the church are all freshly white washed thanks to Walter's folks and the landscapers have brought in some temporary plants that really spruced up the grounds. Kids are wearing their Sunday finest and are working as ushers and valet parkers.

I'm putting on Mabel's dress in the little room in the back that we use for storage. Mother Barker brought in a full length mirror. When I first looked at myself in the mirror I was speechless. I really couldn't believe it was me.

"Angel, Walter is a very lucky man, that's all I can say," Aunt Mabel says as she fluffs up my long trailer.

"Honey, you're a stunner. My beautiful daughter is getting married." Mother starts to cry again. She's gushing like a water fountain, has been all day. I suppose that's how I'll be when my baby girl gets married.

We hug and kiss and share one of those moments that you'll never forget. A girl only gets one wedding day in her life, after all.

I can hear the quartet strike up *"Here Comes the Bride"* when I get within about twenty feet of the entrance of the church. Father is waiting just outside of the main door to escort me to the altar.

"Ya look great, Sonja. I'm very happy for ya."

I think he actually means it, maybe for the first time in his life he is truly happy for me. I'd like to think so, anyway. It's nice that he is on his best behavior; the last thing I need is a bad scene with my father on my wedding day.

"Thanks, Dad. I love you."

I can't recall the last time I'd told my father that I loved him. I was no more than twelve or thirteen at the time, that's for certain. I think it set him back a bit because he looks at me in a very odd way.

Then he says, "I love ya too, Sonja. I ain't been the best at showin' it as much as I should, but I do love ya."

This is the closest thing I have ever received to an apology from the man who made my life such a living hell for so many years.

I have no time to absorb this minor miracle because my future is waiting for me, poised like a sentinel in the front of the altar.

Walter has his hair all combed back and he is standing very tall. He's proud, that's the best way I can describe him. He looks very handsome in his custom made suit and he is sporting a smile that makes me melt.

Lost in a haze, I'm sure that Pastor Walker said "Will you take this man to be your lawful wedded husband?" and I must have answered "I do" at some point. The whole thing is a wonderful blur that ends all too quickly. Walter kisses me right on cue and that's it.

Sonja Kent is now Mrs. Walter Barker.

Lord in heaven I'm happy. Giddy. I don't think I've ever been giddy before, so full of joy that you feel like you just might burst. I wonder if I will get the chance to feel this way again. Surely this is not the only day that will be this special in my life. At least I hope not.

We all caravan over to the Yacht Club. The place is about a half mile south of Neptune Beach, our old stomping grounds. Carol and I used to sneak in here at night and sit on the veranda and imagine ourselves attending a party with all the rich people. Now I am having my wedding reception here. It's the only time in my life when something I've dreamed about has actually come true.

I dance with Walter for the first time as his wife. We have the floor to ourselves for the first half of the song and then our parents get up and join us on the dance floor. I was dreading this moment but, again, my father pleasantly surprises me. Although he has no rhythm and has not even tried to dance since before I was born, he somehow manages to sweep mom around without tripping, doing something that approximates a slow dance. She is so happy. It was as if, just for a brief moment, she actually had a husband that she was in love with.

CHAPTER TWENTY

We decided to spend our first night together as a married couple in our own home. Tomorrow we are off to Charleston for a week long honeymoon. I am so looking forward to that! I've wanted to visit Charleston since just about forever and I think it makes a perfect honeymoon destination.

After years of saying no now I have to say yes. Walter carries me over the threshold and damn near drops me on the other side. I think it's kind of funny, but he doesn't laugh.

On top of everything else I'm tired, bone tired. I feel like I did the first night we arrived in Jacksonville. Walter has to be exhausted too, but he is determined to do one thing, have sex with his wife.

He is a man possessed. I suddenly feel very small and afraid. "Would you like a cup of coffee?" I ask.

Walter says nothing. He starts to take off my wedding dress. He quickly gets frustrated because some of the buttons are hidden.

I'm not ready to take off the dress yet. I want to be a bride for a bit more before I become a wife.

When I try to back off some, Walter grabs me and spins me around and very forcefully pulls the dress off of me. I hear a tearing sound and fear the worst. I can't look. If the dress is ripped I'll be heartbroken.

I am standing here in the living room of our new home with my beautiful dress lying in a heap on the floor. All I have on are my bra and panties.

"Never done this before?" he asks, knowing the answer.

"You know that I haven't Walter." Now I'm definitely in a bad mood.

I expect that Walter will kiss me, tell me how thrilled he is to be married to the most beautiful girl in the world, profess his true love.

Instead he approaches me like I'm a mannequin in a store and unclasps my bra and pulls down my panties.

I'm naked. I'm being inspected, like a side of beef.

He still has all his clothes on. He walks around me, taking in every inch of me with his eyes.

I'm in shock. I can't speak.

Walter likes this, I think. The power he feels makes him even more intent on having his way with me.

"Still a virgin, huh? I kind of thought maybe you weren't telling me everything." He grabs my arm and pulls me into the bedroom.

"You won't be a virgin for long. Where's your perfume?"

"On the dresser. I haven't had the chance to put everything away yet." He not so gently pushes me on to our bed and sprays me with perfume.

Walter then takes off his trousers and I see his manhood for the first time. It looks like an angry snake.

"Spread your legs," he orders me.

"Walter, honey. Can we slow down a bit?"

He says nothing but forces my legs apart. Then he starts rubbing my vagina with his hand. He is too rough.

"That hurts," I tell him, assuming he will stop.

"Girls like this before sex. What's wrong with you?" He just rubs harder, which hurts even more.

"Walter, I said that…"

Now Walter sticks his fingers inside of me. This is very painful and I try and pull away from him.

"Good girls enjoy their sex. Aren't you a good girl, Sonja?"

"Walter, it would be better if you would…"

I can't speak because Walter has climbed on top of me and stuck his angry snake in my mouth. I can't breathe. What am I supposed to do now?

His is thrusting himself in and out of my mouth. It must feel good to him. I just want to die. This can't be sex.

This is not what Mabel told me about. This is something else. "Now I'm going to put this where it belongs. Down below."

Walter removes himself from my mouth and inserts his penis into my vagina.

I scream in agony. It's very dry down there. Is it supposed to be? This is more painful than surgery. God in heaven, what have I done?

Walter slams into me, over and over. He is building up to something. The sheets are covered in my blood.

Then he moans, yells more than moans, and I feel a hot liquid between my legs. I know what this is but it still makes me ill.

What if he would have done that in my mouth?

Walter is sweaty. He rolls off of me and gets out of bed and walks into the bathroom.

I'm a mess, a bloody sticky mess. I am too shocked, too tired, to move. My crotch is on fire, like someone stabbed me with a knife down there. Pain and exhaustion overwhelm me. I pass out more than go to sleep.

When I wake up I am alone. Last night seems like a bad dream. Did I imagine that horror?

I notice the blood on the sheets. It is my blood. Walter has his trophy. I wonder if he is going to hang the sheets on the line for everyone to see.

I feel dirty, in every way. I've never wanted to take a shower more in my whole life. When I try to get up I'm dizzy, so I fall back in bed. It takes a couple of minutes and a few more attempts before my body responds and I struggle into the bathroom.

The hot water does its work. With each passing second I feel better. I remember that tonight I'll be in Charleston.

Maybe Walter just didn't know what he was doing, I rationalize. We are both new at this and he was excited, after all. All of Carol's lectures to me about how boys are so different from girls, that all they want to do is orgasm, that they are not the 'gentlest of creatures', all of this is streaming through my head.

I sprinkle some powder on my body and also some perfume. I slip into my sun dress, the one I bought especially for this day.

Walter is asleep on the couch. I gently tug at him and give him a kiss on the cheek. He wakes up.

"Coffee?" he asks. "Sure," I respond.

As I'm making the coffee I'm thinking, why did he sleep on the couch? He can soil his bed but not lie in it? But he would let me lie in the mess?

"You look good for a girl who didn't get much sleep."

"The shower helped."

"Sorry. You're not a girl anymore, are ya. Sonja Barker is a woman."

Walter kisses me. He has a heavy beard and he has not shaved, or cleaned up at all, since last night.

"Your beard hurts, Walter."

"It doesn't hurt, girlie. Let me know how good this feels."

He shoves me back in the couch and gets on his knees. He pulls my panties down and begins to rub his unshaven face on my vagina.

I'm surprised and shocked, again. Last night was not a bad dream.

"Walter, stop," I say, as forcefully as I can. I scramble away from him, nearly falling over the back of the couch.

"Tell me how much you like it."

"Walter, stop. We're going to be late. We can fool around later."

"We can fool around right now."

Walter has that look in his eye again, like a lion stalking his prey.

He bends me over the couch, pulls my dress up and begins to pound on me; over and over, angry thrust after angry thrust.

It hurts. It hurts real badly.

It takes him longer to finish this time but once more I hear his moan which is more like a yell and I feel the hot liquid spill into my crotch.

He just leaves me there, bent over the sofa and walks into the bathroom.

But before he leaves Walter says, "Clean up this mess before we go, Sonja. What if my mother came over here and saw this?"

CHAPTER TWENTY ONE

My spirits rose as soon as we crossed the Ashley River Bridge and arrived in downtown Charleston. For the last hundred miles or so I had the Walter I knew back, which was a relief.

We didn't talk about our first sexual experience from the time we left the house until we arrived in Charleston. I wanted to, but I thought better of it. I really didn't know what to say.

Just having him back, the boy I loved to talk to, that was enough for me. It soothed my fears that I might have married Jekyll and Hyde.

I kept telling myself that he would be less aggressive after the first few times. He was learning to be married too, right along with me.

The soreness in my private parts reminded me that Walter really needed to calm down, sooner rather than later.

I have never stayed in a fancy hotel. The pictures did not do it justice. The Francis Marion Hotel on King Street was all that, and then some. I'd read the brochure a million times.

It was built in the 1920s when Charleston was regaining its pre-civil war glory. At that time, it was the largest and grandest hotel in the Carolinas. Back then it was "the place to be". While other properties had eclipsed it since then, it was still a magnificent hotel.

"Walter, it's wonderful," I beam as we arrive.

"Nothing like old time Southern charm."

"I agree."

Walter kisses me. It's a nice kiss, the nicest one we've shared since becoming man and wife.

As we step out of the car I grab my husband and shriek like a school girl. "I want to ride on that!" I say, pointing at the horse drawn carriage pulling up to the hotel.

"Of course, Sonja. Whatever you want. This is your special time."

My special time. I sure hope so. Walter and I had not started off well. Maybe this beautiful little city will change all that.

We put away our things in our hotel room. It's not a room, it's a suite! A honeymoon suite!

This morning I felt like a prostitute, now I feel like a princess.

Walter gives me "that look" again, but he does not demand sex. We dress for dinner and leave.

A summer evening in Charleston can be beautiful or it can be oppressive. I am very thankful that the temperatures and the humidity are both moderate. We stroll down King Street and look at all the shops and the beautiful churches. I swear, every Episcopalian in America must live in Charleston! I count five churches in as many blocks.

We eat by the water. It's dark, but I know that Ft. Sumter is sitting out there in the harbor. Tomorrow we are going across the Wando River to see Ft. Moultrie, Sullivan's Island and spend the day at the beach.

Walter is a gentleman all evening. He treats me well; buys me little things, opens doors and pulls my chair out for me when we sit down for dinner. I can tell that he is trying. My spirits soar again. Here is the man I thought I married! We talk about our new house, what we need to do to finish fixing it up and how we are going to deal with this and that subject.

This part of being married I like very much.

The closer we get to the hotel the more Walter's mood changes. He doesn't become rude, he becomes distracted. He is a man on a mission and, I fear, his mission is me.

This time I'm determined to speak up and tell him what I like and don't like, to make sure that he understands that he cannot just grab me and pound on me at will.

Lovemaking involves two people, it seems to me. I'm not an object. I'm a woman with feelings and desires of her own.

Now he is coming out of the bathroom, ready for a romp. He has nothing on. I'm lying in bed waiting for him.

He says nothing to me, but he climbs on top and pins me down with his arms. "Stop," I say, and not in a nice way at all.

"What's wrong now?" he asks, angrily annoyed. At least he does stop. "Walter, I love you. Please don't think I don't …"

"What, I married an ice box? You don't like sex?"

"What we did last night and this morning was not sex."

"It wasn't…how would you know?"

"You forced yourself on me, Walter. I didn't like it."

"Forced myself! You're my wife."

"Yes, I'm your wife. Does that mean…"

"It means that you will satisfy your husband."

"Yes honey, I want to satisfy you…"

"You just need to get warmed up, Sonja. The more you do it, the more you'll like it."

Walter then slides up and sits on my face. He puts his penis in my mouth. I try to say "stop" again, but my mouth is full of him.

"Yea, that's it, Sonja. I like that…oh yeah.."

I try to do something to please him, but I'm about to puke. That would not be good, I tell myself.

He removes his member and slides down my body. Just like yesterday he is tremendously excited and begins to wail away at me like a jackhammer.

"Yea honey…oh yeah.." Walter is having the time of his life, I understand that now. I'm just a prop, a slave to his desires.

Then the yell moan comes. The hot liquid gushes from my crotch. "See," Walter says when he finishes. "Tell me how much you like that!" I'm numb again, in pain. My beautiful day spoiled by this viscous act.

Maybe Walter will hold me now and we can cuddle and talk and try and work this out.

No such luck.

Walter says not another word, turns on his side facing away from me and falls asleep. I'm left lying here in my honeymoon bed with a vagina that feels like someone has poured boiling water on it.

I get up and go into the bathroom. The shower once again partially restores me. I wash myself thoroughly but I realize that tomorrow I have to go to the drug store and find something to treat my injuries.

I'm injured. On my honeymoon. By my husband. I cry.

When I get home I have to talk to Mabel and Carol. They need to help me make some sense of all this, give me the magic words to say to Walter, to make him realize that he is hurting me, not pleasing me.

Then a truly horrible thought forces itself into my consciousness. He doesn't care. All he cares about is himself.

My God. I married my father.

CHAPTER TWENTY TWO

August has suddenly become October. How did that happen? Time is moving at a new pace for me now.

I'm living in a sort of twilight hell, bridging two worlds – the world of Mrs. Sonja Barker, church goer, pianist, newly married wife, up and comer in the Jacksonville social sphere and the world of Sonja the desperate who dreads every night when her husband comes home.

Carol and I are still friends, I guess, but she is two thousand miles away and living her own life. Hearing "I told you so" over and over does not help me very much. Her advice is simple; leave "the bastard", get on a bus and come to California. I considered that for a moment, maybe for more than a moment.

But truth be told I'm not a quitter. I believe in marriage. I believe in God. There has to be a solution. Maybe the solution is just time. If I endure things may get better.

That was Mabel's advice. Endure. I'm not the first woman in the world to have a "randy" husband. I'd never even heard that term, but Mabel says it describes men who like frequent sex. I should be glad, she said, that Walter is "sewing his wild oats" with his wife and not with some tramp.

I should be glad. It's damn hard to be glad. It's damn hard to be nice to a man who could care less how much he hurts you as long he enjoys himself.

Every day, almost without exception, it is the same thing. Walter comes home from work and eats, he might take a nap or read the newspaper, but then he wants me to "perform my duty".

I've learned to do it now with minimum pain and effort. I do not even pretend to enjoy it. I look on it like taking one of my dad's beatings when I was a small girl – just get through it, clean up after and move on. I've taken steps to decrease the pain and I've taken another step as well.

Until Walter proves to me that he can be a good and loving husband I will not bear him children.

I was worried to death that I'd gotten pregnant the first month we were married. Walter had certainly done more than his part to make that happen. I think God intervened, I really do. I'm never sure in life how much is luck and how much is Providence.

At first I lied and told Walter that the jelly was lubricant. I was using it so that I could "enjoy myself more". He was all for that because he is clearly not happy that I am not responsive, that I consider his lovemaking harsh and selfish and that, at this point, I have no desire to sleep with him at all.

But today he discovered the truth. I left the tube out on the counter and he read the label. My timing was pretty good, in a backwards sort of way, because we are headed out the door for church.

"What the hell is this?" Walter says, shaking the tube at me.
"Did you read the label?" I ask.
"Yes Sonja. I read the label."
"Then you know what it is."
"Don't be smart with me. You're using contraception? My wife is using contraception?"
"Yes. You know why too, Walter. Don't look at me like this comes as a total shock."
"I have no idea why my wife would commit such a sin."
"A sin…Walter, let's go to church. We can talk about this later."
"We will talk about this right now."

"Fine. You're a brutal, uncaring man. I do not want to have children with you until you make up your mind to change."

I had never spoken so directly and harshly to Walter before. He was clearly enraged by my tone, but also stunned that those words came out of my mouth.

We went to church, played the music, made nice and said not another word to each other until we got home.

They couldn't see me. I went to the McCutcheon's next door to borrow a cup of milk, but I used the back gate. When I returned by the front I heard my father and Walter talking. I stood behind the fence where they couldn't spot me and I listened.

"Sonja is refusing to have children."

"What did ya say?"

"Your daughter does not want to give you a grandchild."

"Walter, how do ya…why?"

"She uses contraception. She's been doing so for a while now."

"That don't make any sense."

Walter and my father continue to wash Walter's car in the driveway. They usually do this together on Sunday afternoons. It's their time to talk.

"I don't think she loves me, Jerry."

"That don't make no sense either."

"Sonja, she has a mind of her own."

"Told ya that before ya married her."

"She isn't real affectionate."

"She ain't doin' what's she supposed to do?"

"Just."

"You ain't been married all that long. Give it some time."

"I'm not saying you didn't raise her right."

"I sure as hell did – raise her right, I mean."

"I know that."

"Women have to be led. Especially ones like my daughter. Ya know, the ones that think they have somethin' to say all the time."

"That's how it was with you and Faye?"

"Nah. Not so much. Faye doesn't give me a lot a lip."

"What's your secret to marital success?"

"There can't be but one ruler and it's gotta be you."

"Easier said than done."

I feel kind of low and sneaky eavesdropping on them, but it just happened, I didn't plan it. So Walter thinks I'm a bad wife. Well, so much for that. Wonder how he'd feel if I told my father that my husband treats me like a farm animal.

The sad thing is, my father probably wouldn't care.

CHAPTER TWENTY THREE

It's my birthday, December sixteenth. Mother gave me a wonderful present, a beautiful sweater that I had been admiring in her Spiegel's catalog. No doubt the money for the sweater came from her secret stash under the sink.

Mom and I have grown closer since I got married. I'm not sure why, but when I was living under her roof there seemed to be some kind of competition between us, but I was never sure what we were competing for. Certainly not for my father's affection because all I wanted that man to do was stay away from me.

Now I find myself feeling the same way about my husband. Despite my best intentions things are just getting worse.

The sex has not changed. Just about every day, some days even Walter is too tired, I'm subjected to what I can only describe as torture.

I read about women in magazines like *Cosmopolitan* and *The New Yorker*. They talk about how much they enjoy sex. Carol says she loves it. What would that be like, enjoying sex?

Actually I'm sick of thinking about it. The whole subject now is one giant bruise both in my mind and in my crotch. I've tried everything, lubricants, jelly. You name it, I've tried it. Nothing seems to help. It still hurts every time Walter humps me.

I used to hate that term, "hump". Boys use it in a derogatory fashion, bragging that they "humped" this girl or that girl. But that is the best way describe what happens to me almost every single day, sometimes twice a day. I get "humped".

And this husband of mine, who uses me as his own private pleasure pot, what does he give me on my birthday? Nothing. He has clearly forgotten about it or, which could be true and would be far worse, he knows what today is and has chosen to not acknowledge it.

But that's not the worst of it, my birthday woes. I'm sitting here in my living room reading a wonderful birthday card from my brother Luke. I do miss him. We just don't have any time to spend together anymore.

A week ago he ran away from home. Today mother called and she said that the police found him down at the bus station begging money for bus fare to go anywhere.

She let me speak to him for a moment, although I guess my father had forbidden him to talk with anyone. I can't imagine what type of whipping he took from my father…well, truth be told, I can imagine it and it's horrible.

Luke said to me, "It's hard to be a slide rule when your father is a bulldozer."

I asked him what in the world he meant by that and he told me that nothing he does is ever good enough. Luke wants to go to college and become an architect or an engineer. He has a lot of creative impulses, which I think is a great quality for anyone to have, man or woman. Father wants him to be an automobile mechanic. He sees Luke as a working man, or that's how he chooses to see him. If Luke were to become something better than he was that might just kill him. That's so sad.

All of this got me to thinking. Why do people have to be so damn cruel? How can someone justify hurting people they supposedly love just to get their way? Is money that important? Is sex that important?

Where is Jesus Christ when people do such hateful things? I can't find Him there and I've tried.

I will pray for Luke and try and spend some more time with him but the truth is my hands are pretty much tied. He has to gut it out at home for a few more years. I feel for him because I've been there.

My particular hell is that I went from the frying pan into the fire. Thanksgiving did not go well.

My family and the Barkers might as well be from different planets. Not that my in-laws are particularly snobbish, they're not that rich, but they definitely do have manners and ways.

My mother and my mother-in-law do not get along. I'm sure that there are more than a few reasons for this, but first and foremost is probably me.

No doubt I fit the bill in my mother-in-law's mind as a suitable wife for Walter in many ways – I'm a church going woman, chaste, attractive, musically inclined and I can carry on a conversation with most. But she can tell that things aren't quite right between her son and I. I have no doubt that Walter has complained to her about me; he probably does so now on a constant basis.

My mother always sticks up for family, whether it is my father, my brothers or me. At Thanksgiving my mother-in-law must have made some unkind remark about me outside of my presence. When I walked back in with my hands full of pecan pie all I heard was my mother's comeback, "He ain't no perfect angel either, honey."

They were icy cold to each other for the rest of the day. My parents left as soon the dessert was finished.

As soon as the door closed behind my folks the not so gentle grilling from the Barkers began. Am I fixing up the spare room for a baby yet? What do I want first, a boy or a girl? No one came out and plainly said it, but their comments were not subtle. The message was simple – get with it Sonja.

I was polite and played the game. I am living a lie, but that's just the way it is for the moment.

What I really wanted to do was to take my father-in-law aside and ask him if he thought it was okay for his son to abuse his wife.

I wanted to ask him if he treated his wife that way. I wanted to ask him if the family dog deserved to be treated that way.

But I was on shaky ground with the Barkers at the moment for more reasons than my lack of procreative success.

A week ago I went to work at the sporting goods store. They need more help around the holidays and I wanted to give it a try. I missed working at the bank.

It all seemed to be going well until Wednesday afternoon. Ronnie Parsons came in and wanted to buy a new tent. He and his family were going camping at the beach right after Christmas. I had not seen Ronnie since school ended in May and while we weren't the best of friends we used to talk quite a bit.

So I spent a few minutes shooting the breeze with him, catching up with the latest on who was doing what with whom. He even bought some extra items, a fishing pole and some binoculars. I thought that's what I was supposed to do, be friendly and chatty and get the customers to buy as much stuff as I could.

When we got home that night Walter went into a tirade. What the hell was I doing spending all that time with Ronnie Parsons? At first I started to explain, to defend myself, then I just gave up.

When I refused to fight anymore, that's when he blew a gasket.

Did I want to have sex with Ronnie Parsons? he kept asking, over and over again.

What an insulting, stupid, ridiculous thing to say.

Finally I replied, "If I did maybe he would treat me like a woman and not a piece of meat."

I wasn't sure what he was going to do next. Walter hasn't hit me, but I know that he's thought about it. He was thinking about right then, I guarantee it.

So when he turned to go into the kitchen to get Lord knows what, I went into our bedroom and locked the door.

He tried the handle and when it was locked he started to yell and pound on the door. Eventually he broke it down.

When he did he found me lying in bed reading a magazine like nothing had happened.

I wasn't sure what he was going to do next.

Walter took a deep breath, set the door back on the broken hinges and said, "I'll attend to this tomorrow."

Friday was my last day working at the store. Walter told me they didn't need the extra help after all.

It's amazing, it really is, that this man wonders why I won't have children with him.

CHAPTER TWENTY FOUR

My feelings are buried where even God can't reach them.
I have always loved Christmas and appreciated it for it really is, a celebration to remind us that love has come into the world. I'll be the first to admit that there are plenty of people who are a whole lot more religious than I am. But I do believe in Christ and I do believe in love, God's love.

For the past few months I've been begging Him to help me understand my life, to make some sense out of what is happening to me. Pastor Walker assures me that God hears all prayers and that He answers them all of them too, even if sometimes the answer is no, or "not yet", or "you need you to figure it out".

Walter and I worked very hard together on the Christmas musical. Our marriage is a train wreck, but we set that aside for the sake of our church. I don't even see my husband when we play music; I see him as a co-worker, just another member of the congregation.

If nothing else our roles as music team members at The First Baptist Church does give us one place, one outlet, where we are not at odds.

As soon as we get home, everything goes to hell again.

We are locked in some sort of twisted domestic mortal combat. He yells at me if he thinks the dishes have been left in the sink too long. He is unhappy if I use packaged food of any kind to prepare our meals because his mother never uses packaged food. If I take too long in the shower he gets upset, even when I'm in there forever because he has roughed me up and soiled me.

I know what he thinks the solution to all of our problems is, a baby. That I refuse to get pregnant is "the big thing", in his words. All of our" little issues" will disappear, according to my husband, once I'm with child. He even hints that he will "leave me alone" more often once I'm pregnant.

In order to avoid his sexual cruelty I have to get pregnant. Why does that strike me as being probably the worst reason in the world to have a child.

But, it's Christmas. Everyone puts on a happy face and makes nice. When our families are around Walter is very attentive. He even came up from behind me and gave me a gentle squeeze and kissed me on the neck, right in front of his parents.

If he would do more of that when we are alone we might make some progress.

But at least I have a few free moments to call Mabel on the phone and talk in private. She and I have had a couple of conversations over the past few weeks, but I have held back from totally opening up to her.

Not today. She is going to hear it all. Someone has to know. "I didn't know it had gotten that bad, honey."

I laid the whole mess out for her. Now I can't stop crying. "Go ahead, honey. Cry. It's good to cry once in a while."

"I'll be better in a minute. You talk now, I'll listen."

"Seems to me that you and Walter have to come to terms."

"How?"

"I might have to say some things you don't want to hear."

"Go on, I trust you."

"Husbands are to be obeyed, Sonja. That's God's plan."

"I know that, but..."

"Hush. I'm not done. You and Walter should read together what St. Paul says about marriage. He is to treat you will love and respect and you are to obey him. Some men forget the first part. A wife is to obey an *honorable* husband."

"Okay."

"There's more. Your body belongs to him, child. But his body belongs to you. That's how it works. If he's hurting you, it's got to stop. No one deserves to be hurt over and over again."

"Okay." Now I'm crying again.

"But honey. You're his wife. Bearing him children is what a wife does. You cannot tell your husband that you refuse to bear him children."

"I want kids."

"I know you do."

"But I will not bring a child into a house where there is no love. Where God's love does not exist."

"God's love exists everywhere."

"What else can I do?"

"Try and argue less. You're headstrong, Sonja. Don't forget who you're talking to, I know you."

"Yes ma'am."

"Have you spoken with your mother about all of this?"

"I've tried. She says that I should be grateful for all the Barkers have given me.

She thinks I should stop complaining and make my husband happy."

"Faye. God bless her. If Jerry told her to jump off a cliff I swear she'd race over the edge."

I laugh. So does Mabel. It eases the tension just enough. "God has a plan, Sonja. Nothing happens by accident."

"I want to believe that."

"I'm not sure it matters all that much if we believe it or not. I think it's more like gravity. It's just there, regardless."

"It makes it easier if you believe."

"I guess it does."

"I just want to be happy, Aunt Mabel."

"That's what everyone wants, honey. Walter too."

"I think all Walter wants to do is jump on top of me and hammer away."

"He thinks you're pretty. That's not a bad thing, Sonja."
"I wish he was more like Porter."
"There was only one Porter. He was a keeper, for sure."
"I better get back out there or I'll hear about it later."
"I love you, child. It will be okay. Endure."
"Endure. I think I'm getting good at that."
"Better be. You've got a whole lifetime ahead of you." A whole lifetime, I say to myself.

Is it possible? Could I endure this for a whole lifetime? I know the answer. I hope Walter does too.

CHAPTER TWENTY FIVE

"Thank you, Louise."
"You look pale, honey. A drink a water might not be all ya need."

"After church I will ask Walter to...whoa..."

Louise Curtis has to steady me because I'm on the verge of passing out. Right at my piano. In the middle of Sunday service.

Lord no, I say to myself. Not now, not here.

"Honey, I'm gonna go get the pastor, you need to ..."

"Please, I'm okay; only two more songs to go."

With a strength that came from somewhere else I manage to play two more hymns and the service ends.

I'm afraid to look down at the piano bench. I'm sure that it must be covered in my blood.

But my dress is not soiled and the bench is not stained.

I don't think I can stand up on my own. My crotch feels like it's going to explode.

This pain isn't from rough sex, this is something else. Something worse, far worse.

"Pastor, please help her."

Louise brought Pastor Walker over to me immediately after the song ended. "Mrs. Barker, are you ill? You do not look well."

"I think I need to go to the doctor."

"Louise, go get Walter. He walked outside with Mr. and Mrs. Kent."

"Thank you, Pastor. I'll be all…"

That's the last thing I remember before waking up here.

Someone has removed my clothing and dressed me in a hospital gown. My feet are up in stirrups. I'm dizzy and confused and alone in what has to be an examination room.

A nurse appears. She looks over at me and smiles.

"You're awake. Good. Doc will be in to see you in a minute."

"Where am I?"

"East Jacksonville Clinic, right beside the hospital. Your husband and your pastor brought you in, honey. I think your mother is here now too."

"What's wrong with me?"

As if on cue, the door opens and the doctor walks into the room.

"Mrs. Barker, glad you're awake. I'm going to administer some local anesthesia.

Then we can…hold on now."

I try to get up. Not a good idea. My head goes for a swim again.

"Please, Mrs. Barker. Don't move. We need to lance those boils. This is a serious matter."

"Boils?"

"You have blood poisoning in your vaginal area. You had to know something was wrong. It looks to me like…nurse, could you step out for a moment please?"

"Yes sir," the nurse says as she leaves. "Mrs. Barker, I need…"

"Sonja, please call me Sonja."

"Sonja, I have to ask you something. Maybe you didn't want to tell your husband or anyone else, I don't know. Have you been raped?"

"Raped? By a stranger, that kind of raped?"

"Yes. Perhaps, and forgive me for being indelicate, has someone been placing foreign objects into your vagina?"

"Foreign objects?"

"Wood, metal, anything of that sort?"

Suddenly I'm not worried at all about blood poisoning because I know that I will die of embarrassment before anything else kills me.

"I have not been raped," I manage to eke out.

"Sonja, you are suffering from severe vaginal trauma. Something caused it."

"I have only had sex with my husband." Now I'm crying, intensely.

"Your husband did this to you?"

"Yes," I blubber.

"Didn't you tell him that you were in pain, severe pain?"

"He doesn't believe me. He thinks that something is wrong with me because I don't like it when we have sex."

"How long have you been married, Sonja?"

"Since August."

"And you are," the doctor flipped the pages on his chart, "nineteen. Is that right?"

"Yes."

"How often do you and your husband have intercourse?"

"Every day, sometimes more."

"Well, that has to stop. For a while, anyway."

God, thank you for answering my prayer, I scream inside. "Tell him that."

"Oh, I will. Your husband must be made aware that you are seriously ill."

"How serious?"

"If you had waited a few more days and one of these boils had ruptured... Let's just say you were in mortal danger."

"What does that mean?"

"You could easily have died."

Now I really let the tears fly. The doctor holds my hand.

"We caught it in time, Sonja. I'm going to give you a sedative and a local so you will not feel any pain."

"Thank you," I say, between sobs. "Nurse!" the doctor yells.

I don't feel much, a slight prick from the needles – a couple in my arm and another few in my vagina.

I drift off in a bizarre mix of terror and relief.

CHAPTER TWENTY SIX

"Almost done."
"You're very good."
"Thanks. I like being a nurse."
"My friend Carol is studying to be a nurse out in California."
"Is she? It takes a certain sort, that's for sure."
"Sandy, isn't it?"
"Yes, Sandy. Sandy Combs."
"I'm glad this is almost over. The treatments, I mean."
"You are healing well, no complications, but…I should shut my mouth." I reach over and touch her arm. "Please, say what's on your mind."
"You are a beautiful bright woman."
"Thank you." I blush.
"Don't let this happen to you again."
"You talked with Doctor Thompson."
"I read your chart."
"I wish that…I'm afraid." Why did I just tell a stranger that I'm afraid? "Who are you afraid of?"
"My husband."

"He did this to you? I thought for sure that…oh, there I go again, opening my yapper."

"Everyone around here thinks I was raped and didn't report it. You know what, they're right. I was raped. Who do you report it to when you're raped by your own husband?"

"You're my last patient today. Let me buy you a cup of coffee."

"I would love that, Sandy."

We walk from the clinic over to a little coffee shop across from the hospital. The people there know Sandy; she greets all the waitresses by name.

"Come here often?"

"Daily. I'm not much of a cook."

"Not married huh."

"No, been down that road. Not much success."

"Arguing is no fun. I know how that goes."

"That's the least of it. I…I'll leave it at that."

"How long were you married?"

"A couple of years."

"Divorced?"

"Yea, there was no other option really."

"I'm sorry."

"Don't be. Reminds me of a joke my friend Dr. Rex told me. Do you know why divorces are so expensive?"

"I'll bite. Why?"

"Because they're worth it."

We laugh. It's great to laugh again. I think I'd almost forgotten how. "Roger and I, we didn't see eye to eye on things."

"Did he hit you, hurt you?"

"Not any worse than what your husband has put you through."

"Walter has never hit me or anything like that."

"That so. You just told me that he raped you."

"I guess he did. I am his wife, I mean…"

"Why did you say that he raped you if you didn't mean it?"

"I meant it." Sandy is very direct, a quality I like but am not accustomed to.

"Listen, sugar. I'm not trying to give you a hard time. When I look at you, I see me. Well, sort of anyway."

"Sort of?"

"I wish that I was pretty like you."

"You're pretty, Sandy. At least I think so."

"You're a very polite liar and I thank you."

We laugh again. Sandy is unlike any woman I've ever met. She is brash, yet very kind.

"Really, you have a nice shape Sandy, and gorgeous hair."

"My head looks like it's on fire. Carrot top, that's what the kids all called me."

"I've been called worse."

"Freckle face too." Sandy looks at me and "bugs out" her eyes. We giggle so hard that people think we are drunk or something. "Oh, Lord. I need this."

"What?"

"To laugh. It's been a while."

"Life without laughter is empty."

"Lately I feel empty all the time."

"Do you love him? Your husband?"

"I thought I did. I was sure that I did."

"When was that?"

"Six months ago when I married him."

"You've only been married six months?"

"That's it."

"Tell me all about it."

Over the next hour I get to know Sandy Combs. She's from Miami. Her father is a carpenter and her mother is a seamstress. She is five years older than me and has been a nurse for two years. She moved to Jacksonville to hide more than anything else. Roger, her ex-husband, lives in Tampa and is still interested in pursuing her. She has only been divorced for a few months.

"Every time the phone rings or I hear a knock on the door I'm afraid that it's him."

"Why is he still bothering you?"

"Why does the sun rise in the east?"

"You're saying?"

"Roger thinks that I belong to him, that he owns me."

"I can understand that."

"I'm sure you can."

"Have you asked your family to help?"

"My father is getting up there, pushing seventy. He's not in the best of health. I don't have any brothers. I'm an only child."

"My dad is on my husband's side."

"Typical."

"If I needed to I could call the police, I guess."

"Are you kidding?"

"No. Isn't that what the police do, protect people?"

"I might have to take back my 'bright' compliment and stick with beautiful."

By now, even after only an hour or so of getting to know her, I knew that Sandy was kidding, so I did not take offense.

"I'm serious."

"Look, sugar. If a negro jumps you, call the police. They'll be all over that. If your husband, brother, cousin, ex-husband, or any man that has 'dominion' over you smacks you around, they will simply not get involved."

I have to admit it, Sandy is speaking the truth.

In the South the police do not interfere in "domestic" affairs. If a man is assaulted, they will investigate.

If a woman is assaulted, they will investigate and even turn a blind eye most of the time when the woman's husband or father exacts his own justice.

But if a woman is beaten or raped by her own family that is not a matter that concerns the authorities.

"How worried are you?" I ask Sandy.

"I wanted to ask you the same question," Sandy replies. We're not laughing now.

CHAPTER TWENTY SEVEN

"You owe the congregation some personal time."
"Pastor, it's not as if I don't want to be social, it's just that…"
I stop myself before I say something Walter will make me regret.
"It's just what?"
"Walter and I are a …very busy at the moment."
"Oh yes? What's going on?"
I want to tell him that his choir director jumps me usually twice a day, that he assaults me at will without any gentleness or concern for my body, much less my feelings. I want to tell Pastor Walker that Walter is a complete phony; that he comes to church and prays and proclaims the Gospel but then he goes home every night and abuses the woman he promised to love and cherish for a lifetime.
"You're right, pastor. We aren't that busy."
"Don't be shy about reaching out for help, Sonja."
I desperately need help, I say in my mind. Who can I talk to about my problem?
Certainly not you.
"I won't. When would you like us to host the young married couples?"

"Valentine's Day. You two are the most recently married couple in the church. You can be an example to your brothers and sisters, show them how happy you both are, how wonderful it is to be in a committed, Christian marriage."

"Yes, Pastor."

"Us older folks could use a good example too."

"Pastor?"

"Something to remind us that the flame has not completely gone out."

"I get it. Keep the fires of romance burning."

"Yes. You'll see as time passes. A couple can get stuck in a rut and forget to show affection to each other."

God in heaven, I silently pray, let that happen to Walter very soon. "Thank you, Pastor. I'll do my best."

I have lost the ability to speak, to express myself. I think it is probably the very definition of a living hell when you have to suffer in silence, as I do. Even Mabel, my dear, sweet Aunt Mabel, she scolds me as much as encourages me. Everyone is saying to me, one way or another, "Get with the program, Sonja".

Am I the problem? I believe that there are two sides to every story, but I'll be dammed if I can see Walter's side. I've tried. I've thought about our predicament "three ways to Sunday", as Grandpa says.

You know what it comes right down to? Sandy said this to me the other night. No man would put up with the abuse I take on a daily basis. He would hit someone, run away, grab a gun, he would do something.

Why don't I matter as much as a man does? You know what, in God's eyes, I think I do. This belief could very well be my undoing.

"How many showed?"

"I counted twenty couples."

"Wow. I was planning on fifteen tops."

"You've done great, Sonja."

"Thanks, Martha. I think I should re-fill the punch bowl."

"Let's talk a minute before you do that."

"Okay."

"Pastor and I, well, I hope you know how we feel about both of you. Without your music our services would be incomplete. You and Walter are a very important part of our congregation."

"Thank you. We love you and Pastor very much."

"Is there some reason why you and Walter can't have a baby? I just want you to know that you can always talk with me, honey. I'm here for you."

I'm tired of everybody constantly beating this drum. A little chit chat and then it's not good morning, good evening or how's the weather, but why the hell aren't you pregnant?

"Why do you think we want a baby right now?"

"I just assumed that…Mrs. Barker and I talked when we saw each other at the grocery store last week. She said something about you two trying to find a doctor who could help you get pregnant."

"No, we don't need a doctor. All things in God's time, Martha. When the Good Lord is ready, we'll have children."

"Mrs. Barker was so certain that something was wrong."

"I'm fit as a fiddle and so is Walter."

"Glad to hear it, Sonja. Please remember that I'm…"

"Sonja?" Sandy says, as she comes into the kitchen. "You're out of punch, sugar.

Oh, sorry, didn't mean to interrupt. I'll …"

"I was just coming in there to take care of that. Thanks for reminding me." Martha Walker rejoins the party.

Sandy and I step outside. She needs a smoke. "I feel so odd here. I'm the only single gal."

"Have they tried to recruit you yet?"

"Some. I come from a long line of Presbyterians. A Baptist I'm not."

"Don't worry about it. They know that you're here to help me."

"That I am. Everything okay?"

"Other than my mother-in-law is spreading lies about me?"

"This will be good, no doubt."

"Now I'm told that Walter and I are looking for a doctor to help us get pregnant.

Something is wrong with me, I guess. I need medical assistance."

"He really said that?"

"I'm about ninety percent sure. Maybe Walter fed her that bull to keep her off of his back."

"Honey, Walter is…oh, I'm going to shut my yapper before I get in trouble." We laugh.

"Walter is probably wondering where the heck his wife is," I say. "Let him wonder. Don't come running every time he calls."

"It's hard not to."

"Start trying. Change the pattern, change the man."

"Did that work for you?"

"No. But sounds good, doesn't it?" We laugh again.

Walter steps out on the porch while we're in mid-giggle.

"Sonja, we need some more cookies brought out. I didn't know where you were."

"She didn't run away from home, Wally. I'm keeping tabs on her for ya."

Walter looks at Sandy like her wants to slap her silly.

She knows it and could care less. Sandy Combs does not take crap from anyone, especially men.

"I'll get the cookies, sugar. You showed me where they are," Sandy says, as she walks back inside.

Walter grabs my arm as I move to follow her.

"Did you tell her that I don't like being called Wally? Do I have to say something to her? That could be embarrassing for you."

I look down at Walter's hand on my arm. "You're hurting me," I tell him.

"That woman is filling your head with a bunch of trash," Walter says, as he lets me go. do I?"

"She is my friend, Walter. I don't tell you who you should be friends with, now "See, there you go. You only talk like that when she's around."

He's right about that much. But that too has to change.

CHAPTER TWENTY EIGHT

My mother and I have a particular kind of relationship. I know that she loves me and truly wants me to be happy. I want the same for her, but I've never really known what makes her happy. Certainly her children bring her joy, on the whole. Lord knows I've caused her plenty of grief. Luke's battles with my father do nothing but create more misery for her.

We can talk about some things freely and openly, pretty much like two friends.

Mother loves to discuss what's going on in the church, not so much from a gossip as from an information perspective. Faye Kent does not talk crap behind people's backs and that is a quality I have always admired in her. I think I got my intense dislike of gossip from my mother whose view on the subject is simple; if you can't say something nice about someone, don't say anything at all.

Trouble is you can take a good thing too far.

Mother is an ostrich. Now I would never be so rude as to tell her that, but that is exactly what she is. When trouble comes she sticks her head in the sand. She hopes that it will pass so she can pull her head out and look around again without fear.

Not only did I marry my father, something I swore to the Good Lord above that I would never do, I became my mother.

We don't talk about my father or about Walter. Oh we "talk", but we don't really say anything. She tells me that my father is doing this or that, that he is working here or there, that he asked her to do this or that thing, but we don't discuss his arrogance, temper or his pride. All of that is off limits.

I was raised to believe as an absolute principle that a man is the ruler of his castle. Despite everything, my father and Walter and all of the suffering I have and am enduring, I can't say that I disagree with the idea that a man should be in charge of his house.

But we all have limits. Our faith teaches us that. No man, or woman, is without sin. None of us are perfect.

I remember learning the Constitution and The Declaration of Independence in civics class in high school. Now, I mix the two up, but I'm sure that somewhere in there it says that we Americans believe that man is endowed with "inalienable rights" by God to pursue "life, liberty and happiness" if I recall the words correctly.

Until around forty years ago a woman could not even vote in this country. What rights do I have? Not on paper or in some textbook, but in real life? What rights does my mother have?

I'm considering all of this as I'm drying the dishes at my parent's house. Walter and my father are out back "chewing the fat" which translated means complaining about me.

"Mom, how often do you and dad, you know, do it?"

"Sonja! Why would you ask me such an impertinent question?" Mother is beside herself.

I knew she would be, but I asked anyway.

"Because Walter is after me every single day, sometimes two or three times a day."

"That is a matter for you to discuss with your husband."

"Why can't we discuss it? I'll bet the men do, discuss it, I mean."

"That's up to them. Sonja, what's wrong, honey?"

"I don't like being Walter's sex slave, that's what's wrong."

"The Barkers have given you a lot, honey. A nice house, a good life and a very respectable name"

"Money only means so much and besides it's not like I ever see any of it."

"We've discussed this before." This is mother's cue for me to change the subject. "Does Daddy ever hit you?"

"You know that he does not hit me, Sonja."

"Well just suppose he did. What would you do about it?"

"What has gotten into you, child?"

"I'm just trying to make sense of some things."

"You have a good husband and a nice, comfortable life. In return you should do your best to make him happy."

"Do you ever regret marrying Dad?"

"Alright," Mother says, slapping the dish rag against her leg. "What is wrong with you?"

"I'm just going through a rough patch, I guess."

"You want to take your mind off of your problems? Have a child, works every time."

"Did it work for you? Is that why you had kids, to take your mind off of your problems?"

Walter and my father come to my mother's rescue.

"Were going down to the store," Walter pronounces as they walk into the kitchen. "Jerry needs a new shotgun. We have a few of last years' models in the back that I'd like to show him."

"Great," I say.

I can tell that my mother wants to shout something like, "Take me!"

But she's stuck, forced now to answer more "impertinent" questions from her sassy daughter.

The men leave and we finish drying the dishes in silence. Mother makes tea, something we both love to drink after a meal.

I'm set to return to my bold line of questioning when Mom speaks up. "You've got some lofty notions in your head about marriage, Sonja."

"I do?"

"Mabel, she tells you what she wants you to hear, not the whole story."

"What's Mabel got to do with Walter treating me like a field hand?"

"I know how she paints the picture. She and Porter were the perfect pair. They were all smiles and kisses, best friends, all that."

"You're saying that's a lie?"

"No, they were happy, I know that's true. But he was no angel, not all the time.

Not like Mabel tries to make everyone believe."

"What do you mean?"

"Porter liked to drink, for one thing. When he drank too much he would sometimes stay out all night."

"He cheated on her?"

"I don't know. Mabel thought he did, on occasion."

"I don't believe it."

"You don't? People aren't saints, Sonja. Especially men."

"Porter cheated on Mabel? How could you…"

"He hit her a few times too when he was drinking. Not bad, but he slapped her around some. That's for sure, I know he did that."

"She never told me."

I am not happy to hear these revelations.

But if mother is telling me these things then I know they have to be true. She does not make up stories about people, ever.

I want to believe that Mabel and Porter were something special, something different, something I could aspire to be.

"Don't you ever tell Mabel that I spoke with you about Porter, about the bad stuff.

I mean it."

"I won't."

"They loved each other very much. I just want you to see the world for what it is, honey. It ain't perfect. Don't expect it to be."

"Life's a gift, I know that. I do consider my blessings."

"As you should, Sonja. You could do a whole lot worse than Walter Barker." I consider that for a moment as I sip my tea.

Anything could be worse, that's certainly true. My God, I suddenly realize.

It could get worse.

CHAPTER TWENTY NINE

"I can't believe you did that, sugar," Sandy says. "Why not? It's ridiculous," I argue.

"Not it's not. I mean, I don't hate them, not at all. I just don't want to…"

"Sit by them? Negroes are people, Sandy. Just like you and me."

"They're not just like you and me, they're Negroes."

"You and I talk all the time about how women deserve better protection, more rights, all that. Doesn't that apply to Negroes?"

Sandy clams up. I can tell that I've touched a nerve. I tend to do that to people, and not just on occasion. "I suppose," Sandy says, sheepishly.

"The man needed a place to sit down. A seat was open next to me. I didn't know that…"

"Wait. You didn't know that Negroes aren't supposed to sit next to whites on the bus? Especially not a colored man sitting next to a white woman, I mean …"

"Of course I know that, but the bus was full. I didn't think it was a big deal.

Once or twice in Augusta when the bus was …"

"Don't you read the newspapers?"

"Yes, I read the newspapers. I know about all of fighting over this in Montgomery and Atlanta. I think it's stupid and cruel. I'm not afraid to sit next to a colored person on the bus. Are you?"

"Well, no. I guess not. I treat their injuries every day; help them when they are sick."

"There you go," I pronounce. I'm not much of a moral crusader, but some things are just plain ignorant. It's time for the South to grow up. We don't live in the nineteenth century anymore.

We stop talking and take bites of our delicious carrot cake. Sandy loves this little café down by the Jacksonville pier. We often eat here on Saturdays when we go window shopping.

"You embarrassed the poor man."

"I know. I do feel about that."

"The bus driver almost threw us off."

"Really? It was that serious?"

"My beautiful friend, you're clueless."

"All looks, no brains. What can I say?" Laughing breaks the tension.

There isn't much tension to break because Sandy and I can disagree without being disagreeable. We certainly do not see eye to eye on everything. I like it that way. So does she.

"Up North they don't handle things the way we do down here, all this forced separation of races, I mean."

"I do know that much, Sandy."

"Segregation, I have to admit that I like it but I also hate it."

"What do you like about it?"

"If you were a nurse you'd understand what I like about it."

"Well, I'm not. So you'll just have to tell me."

"These colored people…most of them don't have good jobs, so when they need medical treatment they are desperate. I guess I see the worst of it. You know the real hard luck cases."

"How are they different than white people who need help?"

"They just are."

"What do you hate about segregation?"

"I agree that it's unfair. I mean why can't a colored woman sit right here with us and have a piece of cake?"

"What if she did?"

"Then the restaurant manager would ask us to leave. If we didn't he would call the police."

"I guess it has just never been a big deal to me. I really don't think about it too much."

"I don't either. Does that make us bad people?"

"Just Southerners, I guess. We do what we can."

"The other day…it's funny that we're talking about this."

"What happened?"

"A nice young family, a colored family, came into the hospital. Their little boy had cut up his hand pretty bad. He needed fifty stitches to close the wound. Anyway, they were talking to Jeannie, our colored nurse. I overheard what they said."

As I take another bite of carrot cake I notice a Negro man stepping off the sidewalk to let a white woman pass by. This is a common, everyday practice that I just take for granted.

"They were traveling to Mobile from Richmond. They said that Jacksonville was the first place they'd stopped where they could get a motel room. They had to camp out on the way here and be sure that had enough food and water with them at all times because they could not be sure if anyone would serve them."

"I guess I thought that there were plenty of places for Negroes to buy things."

"Me too. These were good people, well dressed. I think the man was a professional of some type, maybe a lawyer."

"I really like the way a good Negro Gospel choir sings. I've seen a few perform, but never in their churches."

"Same God, different churches."

"Yea, Walter and I have talked about it. We admire their musical talents."

"Does Walter have strong opinions about Negroes?"

"If he does, he never shares them with me."

"I'll bet your father does, have strong opinions, I mean."

"You'd be surprised. My father came back from the war with a different point of view. Now, I don't see him marching for civil rights anytime soon, but he has a healthy respect for the colored race. He told me that 'they bleed red too'. He doesn't hate Negroes, not at all."

"What if a colored family moved in next door to him?"

"That might not go over too well. Walter's dad, Nelson, he about had a heart attack when a colored family moved in three blocks away from us."

"Really? Why?"

"The whole idea of it, I think. Nelson sure wants to sell the colored folks tents and sleeping bags and baseball mitts, but he is the most racist man I've ever met. Talks about the subject constantly, how the 'South is going to hell in a hand basket' with all of this civil rights 'bullshit'."

"I guess I have to say it is not a subject I care too much about."

"Me either, but I think I should."

"We have enough to worry about."

"I guess we should thank our lucky stars."

"Meaning?"

"What if we were both female and black? Then where would we be?"

CHAPTER THIRTY

"I just don't know how long, Walter. Grandma Mary broke her leg in three places. She's going to need my help for a while."

"What about me?"

"You're a grown man, you'll be fine."

"As if you care anyway."

Walter is right about that, but I will not give him the satisfaction of admitting it.

"Would you like me to say no? Sorry, I can't come?"

Walter is trapped in a box and it delights me. He cannot say no. If he did, he would look like a selfish cad to his family and friends. I'm sure he's tried to think up any legitimate reason to keep me from going, but there simply isn't one.

"We can't say no," Walter says.

Outside I keep a straight face, but inside I'm grinning from ear to ear. "Will you miss me?" Now I'm messing with him and he knows it. "Sonja, you should really think about…"

"What is it I should think about, Walter?"

"What you say to me, that's what you should think about."

I'm having a ball poking at his tender spot, but I have to quit. I hear a horn blow outside. Mother has arrived to give me a ride to the bus station.

"Will you grab my bags, honey? Thanks."

Walter picks up my suitcases and we walk out to meet my mother. "Call me every night, Sonja."

"I'll try. You've got the number, you can call me." We kiss.

I don't like kissing my husband anymore which is very, very sad.

What's not sad is that for the next two weeks plus I don't have to spread my legs for him.

I might actually not be sore all the time. Imagine that.

"Give my best to Mary," Walter says as he smiles at my mother and waves goodbye. He's a master at putting up appearances.

This time I'm sure about what to do and what not to do on the bus.

However, the last thing I'm thinking about right now is the plight of the Negro.

I'm thrilled that I'm on my way back to Augusta to see my Grandparents. I love them very much and I know that pretty soon they won't be around for me to visit anymore.

The bus is equipped with a set of big fans. Combine the mechanical breeze with the brief spell of cooler weather we've been enjoying and the ride is very pleasant.

We're hugging the coastline; headed to Savannah where I have to switch buses after a brief wait in the station.

I hope the ride lasts forever. For the first time in a long time I feel free and at ease. There will be no tension tonight; no self-pep talks will be required to endure my husband's ritual humping.

We stop at Jekyll Island, Brunswick, then at Sea Island. Is there anything prettier than the Georgia coastline? I let my mind drift and absorb the landscape.

"Sonja?" A man's voice calls out to me as I'm reaching down for a magazine that's stowed under my seat.

I look up and see a very friendly face. "Coach Lewinski," I say. "How are you?"

"Fine and dandy, thanks for asking. How's Walter?"

"Walter is …home," I eke out.

"Mind if I sit?" Coach asks. The young girl who was sitting next to me had just gotten off the bus at Sea Island.

"Please do, I have to switch buses in Savannah."

"I'll be getting off in Savannah as well. Going to visit my kid brother and his new wife."

"How nice," I say, glad for the chance to share the rest of the ride with decent company.

"I ran into Walter a couple of weeks ago at Barkers store," Coach said. "I dropped by to pick up a new baseball glove for my son."

"He's there every day from nine to five," I explain.

"Walter was a very good player. The team hasn't been the same without him."

"He still plays basketball once in a while, mostly down at the YMCA," I offer. "Ya know we had a nickname for your husband, on the team I mean."

"Really?" I had never heard Walter called by any nicknames. "Bulldog."

"Bulldog?"

"Yep, your Walter could get very aggressive when he put his mind to it. I would send him in the game sometimes to give the other team's star player 'the once over'."

"I don't …"

"Get tough with him, ya know, put a body on him."

"Oh," I say. Why didn't I see this side of Walter before I married him? "Yea, you're Walter is a scrapper. I could always count on him."

"He's a 'scrapper' alright." If you only knew coach, if you only knew, I think, but don't say.

But then again, why not say something?

Walter has told me that he looks up to Coach Lewinski and values his opinion. "Coach?" I say. "May I ask a favor of you?"

"Sure Sonja, ask away," Coach answers, as he takes a big swig of his soda. "Would you give Walter a call, or go see him? I'd like you to discuss something with him."

"Sure I will. What do you want me …"

"Walter is very rough with me, Coach. He hurts me. Not just sometimes, but pretty much every day."

Coach Lewinski's expression and tone immediately shift from casual to serious. "Does he hit you, Sonja?"

"I don't want to say …"

"If you want me to go talk with him then I have to know what's going on, at least to some degree."

"He hurt me so bad Coach that I had to go to the hospital. The doctor said…" I can't finish my sentence because I suddenly started to cry.

Coach Lewinski doesn't know what to do now, the poor man. Clearly I have upset him. He hands me his handkerchief.

"Sorry, Coach. I should not dump my problems on to you," I say as I dry my tears.

"Nonsense. I was not raised….let me say this, honey. I'll have a sit down with Walter. You can count on that; he and I will be having a discussion."

Good, I say to myself. Maybe I've finally found someone Walter will listen to, someone he respects.

I don't know Coach Bill Lewinski all that well, but I am aware that he has the reputation of being a no nonsense disciplinarian.

The idea that one of his former star basketball players is mistreating a nice young lady might not sit well with him.

I sure hope it doesn't.

CHAPTER THIRTY ONE

I say that Grandma and Grandpa Kent live in Augusta, but that's not exactly true. They live northwest of the city, near the river. They work their farm and the timber as they have done all their lives. Mt great, great grandparents homesteaded the land and it has been passed down from generation to generation since.

When they die the land will no longer be in the Kent family. No one wants it, at least not as a farm. I would love to be able to buy it just to keep it in the family, but that is unrealistic. I know that my father is counting on his share of the money that he will receive from the sale of the property to be his retirement "nest egg" or to finish paying off his debts, or both.

This is the one place in the world where all of my memories are happy ones.

I consider this for a moment as the young man Grandma asked to pick me up at the bus station drops me off at the front gate.

"I'd be happy to drive ya up to the house," he says, smiling. Is this boy flirting with me? I tell myself to remember exactly what I'm wearing and the perfume I have on because I definitely like the attention.

"No thanks, it's just up the hill. I'd like to walk."

"It was a pleasure to drive ya, Sonja. If ya need anything will yure hear, just holler."

"I will."

A man being nice and kind to me, what a switch.

My suitcases are pretty light, so I grab them and start toward the house. Every step is filled with memories.

When we declared war on the Germans and the Japanese I was just a little girl. War was the last thing I understood. I still don't understand it, how men can just pick up guns and start firing at each other, but that's another story. What I did know is that my father had to leave home to fight in the war.

I lived here for four years. They were, by far, the best years of my life.

During those four years I never heard anyone speak in anger. I was not beaten or berated or discouraged. I do not recall ever feeling anything but loved.

Grandpa Lester was still a strong man back then who did a full day's work.

Sometimes he would take me with him, when it was possible and he was able.

Walking around the turn past the pecan trees I can see myself as a little girl sitting on the buck board of Grandpa's old wagon. The sun is shining, but it is October so it's cool. We have a wagon full of vegetables that Grandpa bought from the local farmer's market.

I see Grandma Mary waiting for us on the front porch wearing that same old grey dress she wore, day after day. It wasn't until later that I learned that she owned five of the same dresses and that she wasn't putting the same one on over and over again. When I close my eyes and think of my Grandmother she is wearing a grey dress and she is smiling.

My father, and my mother too, I guess, think of Lester and Mary as simple people. "Country folk" is the common expression. No one wants to be country folk anymore and live on a farm and make a living off of the land. Everyone wants to a get good job in the city and live a busy, complicated life.

Lately I've been considering the very real possibility that "everyone" might be wrong.

When it comes right down to it I know one couple, two people, who are truly happy; Grandma and Grandpa Kent. When I say happy I mean that they are content with what they have and they are at peace with themselves and with the world.

Now, I don't want to live in the woods either, not all the time. I like the city and its charms, but coming back here once in a while is something I would love to do for as long as I live.

It is something I need to do right now. Being here is a very timely blessing. "Hello child!" Grandpa yells as he sees me walking towards the house.

"Hi Grandpa," I say, in the tone of a six year old girl. I'd like to be six again, at least for today.

"How was the ride in?"

"The best."

"Grandma's been expecting you. She hates the damn wheelchair. Even though it's only for a bit, not permanent like, she hates a gettin' in it."

Grandma is waiting for me in the living room. Their "parlor", as they call it, looks exactly the same as it always did; nothing has changed in my lifetime. Same old brown couch with a sagging cushion and a worn left armrest, three wood chairs, un- upholstered but always polished, yellowed white doilies sitting on well-worn oak tables, lamps that look like they could have been made in Thomas Edison's laboratory and, of course, the family Bible.

The Kent family Bible is their greatest treasure. It is far more than Holy Scripture. It contains the names and signatures of generations of Kent's, back to the one who started this farm.

When I was a little girl my grandparents told me, in all seriousness, that if there was ever a fire in the house I was to grab the Bible first and see to its safety and then come back and retrieve them.

"Hello child," Grandma says, weakly. I can tell that she is not feeling well. "Grandma. I apologize for not coming sooner. I'm so sorry about your leg."

"It's my own fault. That rotted old porch board shoulda been tended to long ago."

"Is it fixed now?"

"Sure is," Grandpa explains. "All them old boards have been replaced. Freddy saw to it last week."

Fred Stokes is their closest neighbor. He isn't much younger than Grandpa, but he is very spry.

"It's about supper time. Can I cook dinner for us?"

"Would ya, child?"

Grandpa looks like he hasn't had a decent meal in days.

"You have any ham?" I know that Grandpa's favorite meal is fried ham and eggs. "Store delivered some yesterday."

"Then I'll get right to it."

"Sonja, I know this is a hardship for ya. We are awfully grateful for your help, child."

"Grandma, I love you guys so much. You have been there for me so many times.

Please don't ever think that you are a hardship. Lord knows I could never do enough for you."

"Your husband though. He don't like ya bein' here," Grandpa says. "Who told you that?"

"Faye," Grandpa admits, sheepishly.

"Mother got it wrong. Walter is thrilled I'm here. He wouldn't have it any other way." Sometimes a fib is called for to protect the feelings of those you love.

"I told you, Lester. You shouldna brought up the subject."

"I 'poligize, child. We just don't want to be no burden to ya."

"No more of that. How 'bout I make some biscuits too, Grandpa. The sour dough kind, the ones you love."

"Sure 'nough. I'm starvin'."

Before I start preparing the meal we pray. Grandpa and Grandma don't always make it to church on Sunday. In fact, if they get there once a month they are doing good, but they always take the time to pray, to give thanks, to remember that God is there and that He is providing for them in all ways.

When Grandpa starts his prayer I close my eyes.

I can hear the announcer on the radio say, "Our boys have landed on Normandy Beach." It is 1944. The world is in a mad frenzy of death, people are being slaughtered by the millions, but I'm here, safe and sound, sheltered in the loving arms of my Grandparents.

Now it's my turn to return a little of that love but, truth be told, as usual it was my Grandparents who are giving the most to me.

I am sheltered again in their home.

Protected from the assaults and insults of a man who should love me as much as they do, who should be my protector, but who has become my nightmare.

CHAPTER THIRTY TWO

"I'd like to talk about it."

"Ain't no one else around, Sonja. Ya know I can keep secrets."

I'm polishing Grandma's silver tea set, which was gift from my father. He brought it back from Europe for his mother when he returned from the war.

"Walter and I are not doing well."

"That ain't no secret, child. Just so you know."

"My parents have spoken to you about it?"

"Your folks and some others."

"Well, give it to me straight. What do they say?"

"They say that you are refusin' to have children with your husband. People are wonderin' why."

"It's true. I do not want children with Walter. Not right now."

"Why not, child?"

"This isn't easy to talk about, Grandma. I mean you and I are …"

"You think 'cause I'm pushin' eighty that I don't understand young folks?

Please. Ain't nothin' new under the sun."

"Walter is not a nice man. He treats me like dirt."

"Be specific, dear."

"He wants to have sex every day, but not sex really. He just wants to jump on me and do his business and be done."

"Yea, men can be pigs. In that department, I mean."

"You know I had to go to the hospital a few months ago, right?"

"Blood infection, ya told me."

"I had to go because my vagina was covered in boils from his abuse. The people at the hospital thought for sure I'd been raped."

"He was hurtin' ya?"

"He didn't and doesn't care if he hurts me. I'm nothing but a piece of meat to him."

"Did he know how seriously you were hurt?"

"Neither of us did, but I told him I was in pain. He would not stop or even slow down."

"And this is still goin' on?"

"Yes. That's why he is upset that I'm here with you and Grandpa. No sex for a while. He's probably going crazy."

"I didn't know it had gotten that bad, child. I'm sorry."

"You being sorry don't change a thing though, does it?"

"No child, 'fraid not."

"What should I do? I don't even want to go home."

"Ya hafta go home, Sonja."

"I know."

"Can ya talk to your pastor about this problem?"

"Are you kidding? I'm the only problem in his mind."

"Has Walter hit ya?"

"Not yet."

For the next few minutes we stop talking and keep polishing. I know that Grandma is thinking about what I've told her. Thinking and praying.

"I need to sit down, child. I can only stand for so long in this damnable cast." I make us a fresh pot of coffee and we sit at her kitchen table.

"Sonja, honey, I want to tell ya somethin'. But you need to swear to Jesus that you won't repeat this to anyone, especially to your parents."

"Sure, Grandma."

"When I was young, before the First World War started, there was someone else.

Another man in my life, I mean."

"You were married to someone else?" The thought of that almost makes me sick to my stomach.

"No, we never tied the knot. We shoulda. I loved him like sin, child."

"What was his name?"

"Ronald Cantwell. He was a Virginia boy. His father was a builder. Homes and such, fancy homes. He was down here for a summer building some mansion."

"What happened?"

"Ronald courted me, very properly. We met at a dance in the old theater. You're too young to remember but once upon a time we had a great outdoor theater here in little old Augusta. Burnt to the ground in 1923. Dang shame.

"Anyway, Ronnie and I was smitten. We had no intention of waitin' to be married. We were sneakin' off no more 'en two weeks after we met. Motels, the woods, anywhere private."

"Grandma!" The thought of my Grandmother as a lustful young girl upset me. "What? Ya think sex got invented by your generation? People are people child, age don't have nothin' to do with it."

"I don't understand. Why didn't you two get married?"

"Woulda, but my father put a stop to it."

"Why?"

"Ronnie's Grandfather was a Negro. Now ya couldn't tell it by lookin' at him. He had blonde hair for heaven's sake and a very light complexion. Both his parents looked white, hell they were white. Someone told my father about it, I'm still not sure how he ever found out. Secrets like that have a way of surfacin', sooner or later."

"Did you care? That he was a Negro, I mean?"

"Heavens no. He weren't no Negro either, child. One eighth blood don't make you colored. Ideas like that are so stupid, so old. Even back then anyone with a brain knew how stupid such nonsense was."

"But my father, your great-grandfather, ya gotta remember he was a boy during the Civil War. He lost three uncles and his own father was wounded, terribly. For him, the old ideas never died. He didn't hate the colored race, but he definitely believed it was a sin to go mixin' blood."

"Ronnie and I, we almost ran off. We was all set to do it, but then his folks got real upset. They were offended. They called my folks 'crackers'. It got ugly real fast.

"One day Ronnie was gone. He left me a long letter sayin' how much he loved me but that he couldn't go against his folks. Broke my heart, child. Still breaks my heart."

"I'm sorry, Grandma." Even after the better part of five decades I can see that this memory is still fresh, the wound has never fully healed.

"A week after Ronnie disappeared and wrote me the letter I noticed I was late.

Went to see the doctor. The ol' rabbit died."

I about drop my cup of coffee. Am I hearing what I think I'm hearing?

"You got another aunt, child. She lives in Atlanta. She's in her late-forties now, has three beautiful kids. She teaches school."

I don't know what to say. I try to let it all sink in without fainting.

"Father sent me away to live in Mobile with his sister. I had the baby and gave it up for adoption. Wasn't supposed to know, but I made sure I knew where the girl lived, her name, all of that. Had to know..."

Grandma is crying. Not hard tears, just a few sincere, sad drops. I reach over and take her hand.

She smiles at me.

Lord in heaven I love this woman.

"I told Lester the whole story before we got married. We ain't got no secrets between us. I love your Grandfather with all my heart and soul, child. I'm so glad I married him. If I hadn't, wouldn't be lookin' at you right now, would I."

"Have you ever spoken to your...your daughter?" It's hard just to say the words. "Never. Won't neither. I figured if someday she came knockin' on my door I'd say that it was God's will but it ain't my place to go messin' with her life. I keep general tabs on her, that's all."

"Can I ever…"

"No child. This is a past thing. Need to let the past be the past."

"Why did you tell me this?" Part of me, most of me, wished she hadn't.

"To let ya know that things just happen in life sometimes. Ya gotta do your best with what ya got. Ya ain't the only woman that's had to make hard choices when it comes to a man."

I nod. I recognize wisdom when I hear it.

"But most of all," Grandma Mary takes both of my hands in hers and looks me straight in the eye, "to tell ya that God loves you, child. He is always there, even at the worst of it. I know this because when I had that baby, held her in my arms and then gave her up, a big part a me wanted to die. I felt lower than dirt. But God lifted me up, gave me hope. I did right in a bad situation, which is a damn hard thing to do, Sonja. Do right and you'll get through it. Do right and God will lift you up."

We pray.

I hope that some of my Grandmother's strength has been passed down to me. Some of her love.

I don't feel so alone anymore. But I'm still scared.

CHAPTER THIRTY THREE

I've been at my Grandparents' house for two weeks and three days now. While she is still hobbled, Grandma is moving quite well. They changed her heavy cast to a lighter one and gave her a set of crutches.

When they took the wheelchair away Grandma was disappointed. I think she was intent on breaking it into little pieces and burying it in the garden.

Yesterday I went to see Miss Bloom. I've visited her three times since I've been here. We are no longer teacher and student; now we are just two old friends.

The pure joy I feel when we play music together is beyond words to describe. When I'm with her part of me "switches on" is the only way I can describe it. I don't consciously read the music or play the notes, I simply express myself. I become a part of the piece, a very intimate part. I don't imagine that I am anywhere else, I am fully present, body and soul.

When I am with Miss Bloom all that exists is the piano and our friendship.

She plans on coming to Jacksonville for a visit. I hope she does, but what I really hope is that…

I try not to think about what I really hope for.

This is the life I want. To be around people who love and like me without the stress of obligations or husbands. I love Augusta. I miss the life that could have been, that should have been.

Instead of dealing with my husband's relentless advances and the endless questioning of my family and church friends, I should be studying music at college. I should be playing piano with Miss Bloom. I should be...

"Shoulds", I think, are a dangerous trap.

I get caught up in "shoulds" all too easily. If things should be a certain way and they aren't then it is all too easy to feel sorry for yourself, to become a constant complainer, to believe that you are entitled to a life free from challenges and suffering.

What I "should" do is deal with my problems and count my blessings. How much longer can I stall Walter?

He knows that Grandma can get around on her own now. He sent money for a bus ticket home. I bought the bus ticket, but it's open ended. No specific departure date.

When he calls I try not to answer. Every two days, I tell myself. We can talk three or four times a week and that is sufficient.

I'm having all these thoughts on a Saturday morning as I clean up after breakfast. There is a knock – not a knock, a pounding on the door.

Grandma is in the bath and Grandpa has gone to the neighbor's house to retrieve some tools.

I know who it is before I get to the door.

"Hi honey!" Walter says, excitedly. He lets himself in as soon as he sees me. He has a bouquet of flowers in his hand and a box of candy.

We kiss. I feel nothing. He kisses me again. I gently pull away. "What are you doing here?"

"I missed you, Sonja. Came to bring my bride back home, if your Grandma is feeling up to resuming her duties around here, of course."

Resuming her duties, I tell myself. You want me to resume my duty, that's why you're here.

"Come in? Are you hungry? Let me fix you some breakfast."

"Thanks. I could eat."

Walter grabs my backside as I turn away from him. He keeps his hand there as I walk.

"Walter," I chide. "What if Grandpa came back home?"

"I missed you, Sonja."

"Why don't you start with a meal."

I give him a quick peck on the lips, turn and begin to prepare his plate.

We talk about things back in Jacksonville. When Walter is like this, I'm reminded of the man I thought I married. He even makes me laugh once or twice.

Has he changed? Maybe just a little bit? I try and be encouraged.

"Hello, Walter," Grandma says, as she comes into the kitchen, sets her crutches down and sits at the table.

"Hello Mary. How are you?"

"Feelin' better. Your wife sure has been a lifesaver."

"We are thrilled to help."

Walter always says the right thing in social situations. He can turn on the charm at will.

"Didn't know you were comin'. Thought Sonja was takin' the bus back home."

"I missed my wife. I got up at three in morning and started out. I just had to see her."

He emphasizes his sincerity by squeezing my hand and giving me an affectionate kiss on the cheek.

Walter has no idea that my Grandmother knows our whole story and therefore understands exactly why he is here. I'm sure that he assumes I have not told her about our issues.

"Well, always glad to see you Walter. Lester will be back in an hour or so. He would love to say hello and thanks too."

"I heard you got rid of the wheelchair."

"Damn thing is gone, thank the Lord."

"Leg fully on the mend then?"

"Yep. I can get around pretty good now on these sticks."

"So glad to hear it, truly answered prayer."

"Things okay with you?"

"Sure, all is well. It will be, I mean, when I get my Sonja back. I was kind of hoping that I might steal her away this weekend."

"Oh?" I say.

"I booked us tonight in a nice hotel in Savannah. I thought you deserved a break after all your hard work. How about a nice dinner and an evening out with your husband?"

"Walter, that sounds nice." It actually does sound nice; depending upon who I'm dealing with of course – Dr. Jekyll or Mr. Hyde.

"You kids go on. We can take it from here."

"We should wait until Lester gets home, Walter. He would be offended if we …"

"We aren't in that big of a hurry."

"I can start to pack up my things."

"Can I sit here and catch up with Mary while you pack, or do you need my help darling?"

"Talk with Grandma, please."

"I will then. Just let me know when you're ready to go. I'll take you suitcases out to the car."

Lord please let Walter see the light, I pray.

Let this kind, loving man sitting at the table really be my husband. When I talk with him tonight, let him listen to me.

Give me the right words to say.

I am resolved to fight for my marriage.

A big part of our problem might simply be that I have let Walter get away with too much. This has built resentment bordering on pure hatred in me at times.

I need to do better.

Then maybe he will do better. Then maybe we can do better.

CHAPTER THIRTY FOUR

So far, so good.

I made it to Savannah without Walter assaulting me.

He is continuing to be his charming self, the man who dated me and convinced me to marry him, not the selfish, sex crazed fiend he has been ever since I said "I do".

Our hotel is not as fancy as the Francis Marion Hotel, but it's very nice. I'm not expecting a second honeymoon, just a place to relax with my husband.

A place to talk, to listen and hopefully to heal.

My body is certainly in better shape. No more soreness. I had forgotten what it was like not to be in constant pain.

Walter has to show some compassion for me, if nothing else.

Tonight I need to make my husband understand that he was hurting me and, in the process, that he almost destroyed our marriage before it began.

Even though neither of us is old enough to drink, Walter orders wine with dinner. I didn't know that he liked wine. I sip it, slowly. It tastes good, very good. I'm beginning to feel a little tipsy which, I'm sure, is exactly how Walter wants me to feel.

"... yea, pastor actually said that. I mean it floored me. Emily and Martin are just two kids, they didn't know any better."

I take Walter's hand and gently squeeze it. He responds by kissing me. "Let's go back to the room, honey. I've really missed you," Walter says. "Okay."

We walk back to the hotel arm in arm. I'm praying as I walk.

As soon as the hotel room door closes, the Walter I dread comes to life.

It's almost as if he has two personalities. Or does he really have only one personality, the one I despise, the one he masks just to get what he wants?

"I need you, honey."

Walter starts to undress me, pulling off my blouse with too much force. "Walter, we need to talk."

He can't hear me, or he won't hear me. He is intent on humping me. "Sonja, I missed you, I need you..."

"Stop!" I shout and pull away. "What's wrong now?"

"We need to talk, honey. Let's sit here on the bed and just talk. For minute, that's all I'm asking."

"We can talk later," he says, and pushes me on to the bed. He begins to take off his pants.

I stand back up and slap Walter right across the face. It's not a love tap; I give him all I've got.

Walter does not know what to do for a minute. He's in shock. I say nothing.

Then I see it coming.

His rage. His face turns bright red.

Next thing I know Walter hits me. Not a slap, a punch to the jaw.

"Who in the hell do you think you are? Slap me like I'm some sorta ..." I'm dazed, hurt. I feel my dress and then my panties come off.

Walter is on top of me, holding my arms down and then he is in me. I struggle, try to break free, but he has me firmly in his grip.

Walter is hammering on me like a wild animal in heat. He is enjoying this. The yell moan comes and then he releases me.

The whole episode is over in less than five minutes.

Now it's morning. I'm afraid and I'm angry—angrier with myself than I am with Walter.

I hit him first. That is the thought that keeps going through my head. I started it.

Walter just reacted.

When someone gets hit their natural response is to strike back. What the hell was I thinking?

Walter has gone downstairs to pay the bill. He seems calm this morning and he did not come after me at the crack of dawn as I feared he would.

I'm toweling off when he returns. "Breakfast?" he asks.

What do I do now? I need to know. Pretend that nothing happened, run away? "Sure. Are we going out?"

"Whatever you'd like, dear. Room service or we can go to a café."

"Let's go out." I want to be in a public place as soon as possible.

Walter comes up from behind me, kisses me on the neck and gently drapes the bathrobe over my shoulders.

"You should have told me," Walter says. "Told you what?"

"That you like it rough, darling. Look, it's okay with me. Tell me what you want and I'll do it for you."

"You think…I mean…you actually think that I enjoyed what happened last night?"

"C'mon, Sonja. I saw the look on your face when you slapped me. It excited you, made it fun. I'll never tell. I like to play too."

"Walter, I…for heaven's sake…I"

"Just go easy on the face, honey. You left a mark." Walter pointed to his left cheek where my nail had dug into his skin and cut him.

"Walter, my God…you've got to be …"

"You look fine. Not even a bruise."

My jaw was sore, but not swollen.

I'm stunned, incredibly disgusted and repelled by this twisted jerk I married. Inside of me a voice says, "You're not safe in here. Go along with him for now."

"Walter, let's go eat. We can talk about this later."

"Later we can play some more. You might have to punish me for being such a bad boy."

'Punish him?' I think. Who in the hell am I married to?

"Oh, and by the by dear, I talked with Coach a couple of days ago. I know you mean well Sonja, but you need to watch what you say to people. Coach had the impression that I was a wife beater or something. I set him straight, not to worry."

CHAPTER THIRTY FIVE

There was only one person I knew who would understand, who could make some sense out of this insanity.

I had to find Sandy.

It was late on Sunday night and I could not reach her on the phone. I told Walter that Sandy was having some "female problems" and needed my help.

After I let him hump me without complaint he let me go.

As soon as I reached her apartment I knew that something was wrong. The door was slightly open and there was only one small light on in the living room.

I found Sandy wrapped in a sheet and curled up on her couch asleep.

She looked okay, but I knew that something must have happened. I gently shook her. She woke up.

Sandy said, "Roger found me."

"Where is he?"

"What time is it?"

"About eight or so."

"He's probably gone then."

"No one else is here right now, I know that much."

"He had to be home on Sunday, so he took off."

"It's Sunday night, honey."

"No it's not, can't be…"

"You've been lying here for a day and a half. Let's get you up." I help her take a shower.

When she is clean, after I have picked up her house and set her down at the table with a cup of tea, I ask, "Did he?"

"He tried, but he couldn't."

"What do you mean 'he couldn't'?"

"He couldn't, you know, get an erection. He was too drunk."

I am so naïve. "This has to end. Roger needs to leave you alone and move on."

"Roger won't stop trying to get me back. Ever."

"I came to see you because Walter and I…we…" I didn't want to lay my troubles on her; God knows she had enough to deal with already.

"Walter what?"

"Now the fool thinks I 'like it rough'. I slapped him when he wouldn't stop. I'm lost Sandy, so lost."

"What are we going to do?"

That was it. I had my epiphany, clarity of vision. We have to do something.

No one else is going to help us. We have to help ourselves. "It's time that we took charge of our lives, Sandy."

"What does that mean?"

"First thing it means is that we are moving you out of here tomorrow. My friends the Scotts have been trying to rent their back cottage to someone for a month. We'll move you in there. There is no way Roger could get at you even if he knew where you were because the Scott's have five kids and three huge dogs. You're safe at work."

Sandy perked up. "I like that idea. Helps a lot."

"Second thing it means is that I'm done being Walter's pet. I'm giving him a choice; he can get some help, act like a Christian man and treat me like a lady or he can go to hell and he can go there without me."

"Then what?"

"We either straighten all this out here, in Jacksonville, and these men realize that we are not chattel or we leave and start over somewhere else."

"Why not just leave now?"

"I'm not a quitter. I haven't been much of a fighter either, but that changes as of now. As God is my witness I will not be a victim anymore. Not for one more second."

"I'm with you, honey."

CHAPTER THIRTY SIX

"Why are we here?' Walter asks.
"Because we need to talk and not at home," I explain.
"Okay, I guess."
Walter doesn't like anything to interrupt his routine.
He wants to come home from work, eat a meal, take a brief nap and then assault his wife.
Day after day, night after night he repeats this pattern.
It's late July now. I've been married for over ten months. Soon it will be a year, then five years, then …
I can't bear to think about any more "thens". "Walter, you need help."
"Help?" he asks, taking a big gulp of a milk shake.
"Yes, help. You have some serious problems you need to deal with right now."
"Such as?"
"For starters, you're a selfish, brutal bastard." Walter's eyes get wide and his cheeks red. "Sonja, God help me I try and be patient with …"
"Do you actually think that I enjoy you pounding on me night after night?"

"Frigid, I knew it. You're as cold as ice."

Lord in heaven I want to slap him again.

But I knew that I'd feel this way and I restrain myself. "I think that I might like sex, Walter."

"Not with me."

Now he is pouting; first the rage, then the pout—another of Walter's patterns. "What part of you manhandling me and pumping me until your done do you think I enjoy?"

"Well, maybe you're not supposed to enjoy it."

"Just do my duty."

"I do mine, don't I? You have a great house, nice clothes a good life. You can't say that I don't provide for you."

"Did I say that you didn't provide for me? I said that you assault me, that you hurt me. What good are houses and clothes if I'm in pain all the time?"

"You are not in pain all the time."

"So now I'm a liar?"

"You're a woman. You exaggerate, comes with the territory."

"So I guess you figure that the doctor was lying to you a few months ago when he told you I might have died from blood poisoning."

"No, but I didn't do that to you."

"No? Who did?"

"I've wondered about that since it happened. I wonder even more now."

"Are you saying that you think I'm cheating on you?"

"The thought has crossed my mind."

"For God sakes, Walter. You're an ass."

"An ass, huh? Selfish bastard? You're the one who won't give us children and I'm selfish? All you want to do is loaf around the house all day and complain. Bitch and moan. Well, I'm sick of it."

"I'll bet you're sick of it. I know I am."

"Why did you marry me?"

"You did not act like this before we were married. You were sweet and kind and even gentle with me."

"Don't I take you places? Out to dinner, on trips? Most women would love to be so well cared for."

"Most women would tell you to keep your pecker in your pants until you learn to respect your wife."

"My 'pecker'? Who teaches you such foul language? Your slut friend Sandy, I'm sure."

I have to call on every ounce of self-control. I'm determined to stick to the plan.

Calling Sandy an ugly name makes me madder than hell, and he knows it.

But I'm engaging my brain, not giving in to my emotions. Rather than slap him or say something rude back, I smile and declare, "I'm off limits to you, Walter. No more sex, as of right now."

"You're my wife, you.."

"Get help, Walter. Talk to Pastor Walker or a doctor or a friend or somebody. You're hurting your wife. You have one chance left to save this marriage, Walter. One more chance and that's it."

"Now you're threatening me?"

"No, promising you. I married you for better or worse. As mad as I am right now, I'm no quitter. I want you to get help so we can have a chance at a life together, a life with kids, happiness, everything good."

"You're perfect, of course. None of this is your fault."

"I do not hurt you Walter, and I'm not selfish. I'm not perfect, but you are the problem here, not me."

"Sonja, honey…"

"Don't honey me, Walter. Get help." I stand up to leave.

"Where are you going?" Walter asks.

"To Sandy's house. I'm staying with her for the next few nights. You need some time to think about what I've told you."

"You're leaving me."

"Not yet but that's next, if you don't get some help."

"Stop telling me to get help."

There is nothing else to say. I turn to leave.

"Hey," Walter says. "Didn't Sandy move a few days ago? I don't even know where she lives."

"That's right, you don't."

As I walk out of Ozzies Mr. Kearns waves goodbye. I smile, maintain my composure. Sandy is waiting for me around the corner.

I did it, I actually did it. I congratulate myself.

For the moment I'm not worried about what happens next, but I know that I have started something that will not be easy to finish.

CHAPTER THIRTY SEVEN

"Sandy, I forgot to tell you that ..."
"Sonja?"
"I'm sorry, who am I speaking with?"
"This is Pastor Walker, Sonja."
"Pastor, oh, I'm so sorry. My friend was going to call me right back...anyway, what can I do for you?"
"I just received a very disturbing phone call from your husband."
"He's working today, or so I thought."
"Yes, he called me from the store. I am very concerned about you two. I figured you might be home by yourself so I called."
"I'm here, by myself."
"Walter says that you moved out, left the home."
"No, Pastor. I stayed with my friend Sandy for a few days. I came back last night, but I moved into the spare bedroom. I bought a lock for the door."
"We need to talk about your marriage, Sonja. Walter is beside himself."
"What has he said to you?"
"That you are very angry with him."
"Did he tell you why?"

"I think it comes back around to the same issue, children. He is concerned…"

"Children? That's amazing."

"That's not the issue?"

"The 'issue' is that I am sick and tired of being his sex toy, Pastor. Do you want details?"

"Is Walter asking you to do something sinful in the bedroom, Sonja?"

"Sinful?"

"I don't want to get too explicit with you, but if he wants you to do things…"

"He wants me to lay there and take it, to be available for his pleasure whenever he wants to hump on me. He hurts me, Pastor. He is very rough. He treats me with disrespect too, the other …"

"But is he asking you to do something sinful?"

"Isn't it a sin to be mean and brutal to your wife? To treat her like an object?"

"It is a sin not to bear your husband children. That is your duty."

"Walter slams me down on the bed, or bends me over a chair and pounds away at me. He does this for his own pleasure. I don't get a kiss, a hug or an anything. I'm nothing but a piece of …"

"Have you discussed this situation with the Barkers?"

"You're kidding, right? As far as they are concerned Walter walks on water.

They don't want to hear about our problems; or rather, my problems."

"Have you two brought this before the Lord in prayer?"

"God is love, isn't that right?"

"You know He is, Sonja. God is pure love."

"If God is love and my husband is supposed to cherish me, how can you ask me about 'sin' in our marriage? Start with …"

"You need to be careful in these matters, Sonja. We all have duties – me, you, Walter, all of us."

"What is my 'duty' to God in my marriage, Pastor? Tell me what God wants me to do."

"He wants you to love your husband, bear him children and serve the church."

"You don't care, do you."

"Of course I care, Sonja. That's why I'm taking this time with you so …"

"Walter is a brute, a selfish brute. As far as you're concerned that is not a sin, so I should shut up and take it."

"You should talk to your husband about your issues in the bedroom and work out your problems in prayer."

"Anything else, Pastor?"

Pastor can tell that I'm dismissing him and he doesn't like it.

"Sonja, you need to seek some help. Perhaps one of the ladies in the church…"

"Are we done, Pastor?"

"I suppose so."

"Thank you so much for your concern."

"Very well."

Walter has told our pastor the story he wants him to hear, that I am a bad, selfish wife who will not start a family. That I complain about everything, especially about having to "properly" take care of my husband.

I wonder, how many other women are in the same fix I'm in or worse? How many of them suffer in silence as they endure everything from simple disrespect to beatings and rape?

I look at the picture of our Savior on our living room wall. What does He have to say about all this?

Seems pretty clear to me.

He stopped men from stoning a woman to death for being an adulteress. His words were, "The one without sin shall cast the first stone." Then He began writing something in the dirt. I've always wondered what He was writing. The names of the women the men in the crowd had slept with out of wedlock? The names of the men in the crowd who had slept with the sinful woman they were about to murder?

Jesus never condoned cruelty or violence, against either men or women. Why do we condone it?

Why is it swept under the rug, or excused?

Why is a wife's right not to be hurt by her husband not an absolute? What's wrong with us?

As Christians we should know better.

CHAPTER THIRTY EIGHT

"Beautiful day."

"Yes it is, Nelson."

"Seems like everyone is out and about spending money this time of year."

"Back to school and all."

"You and Walter coming over for supper tonight?"

"That's the plan."

"Sonja, June and I are concerned."

"About?"

"Your marriage."

"Nelson I, we, are trying to work things out."

"We've never seen Walter so unhappy. That disturbs us."

Bet it does, I say to myself. Now you're going to tell me what I need to do to make things right.

"I don't want Walter to be unhappy."

"Please reconsider your decision not to have children."

"I haven't made any such decision. Did Walter tell you that?"

"He told us that you're sleeping in the spare bedroom behind a locked door and that you've been doing so for a month."

"Did he tell you why?"

"He said that you are angry with him."

"That's true. Did he say why I was angry?"

"No, and I don't think it's our place to pry into…"

"Walter is too rough with me, Nelson. He simply does not care if he hurts me or not and he cares even less about what I need in terms of intimacy."

"Sonja, maybe you should speak with June about this, I'm not…"

"Sorry, Nelson. I didn't mean to embarrass you."

The poor man's face has turned beet red.

I like Nelson Barker. He is a good businessman, he's always been nice to me and I have never seen him treat June with anything but respect.

Makes me wonder where his son learned his bad habits from if not from his father.

"Sonja!" My mother shouts. "Over here mom!" I yell back.

The latest contestant in the "Battle of the Bands" has begun to play. This is an annual event at Barker's Sporting Goods and it always draws a large crowd. I counted over two hundred people milling around in the parking lot. A local radio station hosts the whole thing and provides a DJ and a huge sound system.

"Hi, honey." Mother gives me a kiss on the cheek. "Faye."

"Nelson, how are you?"

"Good. Did Jerry tag along?"

"Nope, it's just me and the kids. Jerry is off working." I give my brothers each a hug and a kiss.

"Ma, Vince and I want a hot dog," Luke says. "Run along then, just stay in the parking lot."

"Tell them who you are so you don't have pay," I instruct Luke. Nelson says his goodbyes and walks off.

"Love that dress," Mother compliments.

"Thanks," I answer. "It was a gift from Walter."

"Peace offering, I hope?"

"Don't you start," I warn. "I'm sick to death of talking about my marriage."

"Couple of ice cubes, you two."

"Hey, root for me! The hula hoop contest is about to start."

"You entered?"

"Why not? Your daughter can swing her hips with the best of 'em"

There are ten of us in the competition. As soon as each contestant starts to hula hoop, the band plays and keeps on playing until the hoop hits the ground.

When it's my turn I notice that Walter is watching me. He has been inside the store all morning, but he knows that I'm entering the contest. Now he is standing out front with his father.

As I requested, the band plays *Rock Around The Clock* when I begin.

My hips keep moving for almost three minutes before I run out of gas and the hula hoop drops to the ground.

"Sonja Barker, two minutes and forty five seconds. How about a big hand for Sonja!" the DJ bellows.

I bow and go to find some water. "Hey there, sugar!"

Sandy made it. She wasn't sure if she be able to switch shifts and come. "Did you watch me?"

"Quite the moves. Think you'll win?"

"Nah. See the girl coming up next? She can go for five minutes, easy. But I had fun."

"Walter is giving me the evil eye."

We both look over at Walter. When we do he turns and re-enters the store.

"Let's sit over here," I say, as I point to the benches set up behind the bleachers. "Well, was it him?" I ask.

"Not sure. Mr. Scott said that someone who fit his general description was poking around, but as soon as he confronted him he apologized, said he was lost and took off."

"Sounds like Roger to me."

"It was only a matter of time."

"Does Mr. Scott know about Roger?"

"I told him all about my wonderful ex-husband."

"And?"

"If Roger, or anyone else, comes on to the property without permission Mr. Scott says that he will have his two friends ready to deal with him."

"His 'two friends'?"

"Mr. Smith and Mr. Wesson."

"Bart Scott is a really good guy," I say. "I've known him and his family since I moved Jacksonville. God bless him."

"Gives me some comfort at least."

"I'm going to hide out over here with you."

"What's going on?"

"Everyone wants to weigh in on my marriage."

"Gets old, does it?"

"Real old, real fast."

"Well, then let me join the chorus. What did Walter say?"

"He said that when I move back into the bedroom then we can talk about all of our issues."

"Give him what he wants and he'll decide whether or not to hurt you some more?"

"That's not how he put it, but that's what it comes down to."

"And you said?"

"'Think again'. I did offer an alternative."

"Oh?"

"There are people out there who offer 'marriage counseling'. I guess they are psychologists, I'm not sure. I thought Walter and I might try going to someone like that, not a pastor, a doctor."

"And he said?"

"'Think again'."

CHAPTER THIRTY NINE

"Who are these folks again?"

"Adam and Alice Hunt. Adam is the pastor of a church in Nashville. He and Pastor Walker have been friends for years."

"You know I like entertaining," which is true, I do like cooking and socializing, "but why are we having them over for dinner?"

"They haven't had much luck organizing a choir. They like our work so they thought we could give them some ideas and guidance."

"Sure we could." I'm interrupted by a timer going off in the kitchen. "Dang it, I forgot to pull those rolls out. Walter could you…"

"Got it dear. Anything else I can help you with?"

"No, but thanks for asking."

Walter is being awfully sweet today. I hope this means that I've finally got his attention and that he is thinking about me, about us.

The distraction of entertaining guests might be just what we need tonight. Something to help us feel normal.

We'll just be a young couple enjoying themselves with good company.

I allow myself to indulge these happy thoughts and smile as I finish putting on my makeup.

After a few minutes the doorbell rings. Walter answers it and I hear him talking with the Hunts.

I emerge from our bedroom and exchange greetings with our guests.

"So nice to meet you both," I say, heading toward the kitchen. "Have a seat in the living room, please. Can I bring you anything to drink?"

"Thanks but no, were fine. You have a lovely home Mrs. Barker," Alice responds.

"Sonja does an excellent job. She has quite the eye as a decorator," Walter compliments.

Wow, I say inside. A month plus worth of silence and pouting and now Walter is complimenting me in front of strangers.

Progress?

I can only hope.

We sit down to dinner and strike up a conversation.

Adam and Alice are ten years older than us. He has been a pastor for five years and this is his second church. Alice stays at home with her three children, the youngest of whom is barely two. They are both from Nashville so they have their families around to help and support them.

After half an hour of very pleasant chit chat no one has brought up the subject, so I do.

"Walter tells me that you need some advice on how to start up a choir."

Adam looks at Alice. I get that they are deciding which one of them should answer the question.

"We have a choir, Sonja, a very good one. It would be nice if you and Walter could come up and visit us sometime and hear them perform," Alice explains.

"Oh," I say. "I thought that you needed some…"

"Pastor Walker asked us if we could meet with you two and perhaps offer you some encouragement and prayer," Adam says.

"So you didn't come over to talk about music?"

"We can talk about music or whatever you like, Sonja. We came over to try and help."

"You knew about this Walter? Why they really wanted to see us?"

"Yes, honey. Pastor Walker suggested that you could benefit from their …"

"That I could benefit?"

"We work with troubled Christian couples, Sonja," Alice says. "You and Walter aren't the only ones who have difficulties in marriage. Adam first had the idea a few years ago, for him and me to become a ministry team, to reach out to our brothers and sisters in need, to …"

"Great," I say, with enthusiasm. "You should have been straight from me from the beginning about why you were coming, but great. Let's talk."

"Maybe we should finish dinner first…"

"Nah, Pastor. Let's talk now. Should I start?"

"Sure, Sonja. Say what's on your mind," Alice says.

"For the first year of our marriage, from the wedding night on, Walter has considered me to be his personal property. His idea of sex is to throw me down on the nearest couch or bed and jump me. He pounds on me so hard, two or more times a day if I let him, that he nearly killed me. I almost died from blood poisoning due to the boils created by his …"

"Sonja, that's not true. I didn't know …"

"Walter, please let your wife speak," Pastor Adam says, interrupting.

"I've tried, for months, to be patient. Things just get worse. Walter can be very nice when he wants to, but I think it is an act to get what he wants – a hump, a lay, whatever. He likes rough sex too. He even had the gall to say that I liked to be hit, that being hurt somehow made me happy in the bedroom.

"I don't know who I married. All I want is to be treated with respect and love. It does not make me happy to say bad things about my husband, nor do I like complaining. But this brutality has to stop. I have the right not to be injured by my own husband."

"Is that all you want to say, Sonja?" Alice asks. "For the moment," I answer.

"Walter?" Adam says, looking at my husband.

"I'm very sorry that Sonja feels the way she does. I want to make her happy. I try to make her happy.

"I like sex. I am very attracted to my wife. From the moment I met her all I could think about was being with her. In a physical way, I mean. It makes me upset that I should have to apologize for being madly in love with my wife."

"Walter, that is simply not …"

"Sonja, it is Walter's turn to speak," Pastor says.

"I provide for her – a home, a car, a good income, everything I can do. It is my duty and honor and my pleasure to do these things. I know that is what God wants me to do.

"I would never hurt my wife. She got sick and blamed me. I don't like 'rough sex', whatever that is. Maybe she got the wrong impression. I want to make her happy in the bedroom, but I just can't seem to do that. Sonja is a difficult woman, very particular and demanding. She exaggerates about everything. She turns every little thing into a major drama. I'm at my wits end."

"Is that all you want to say, Walter?" Pastor asks.

"Yes, I just want some help. I want someone to help my wife."

We all sit in silence for a moment.

I replay Walter's comments in my mind.

For me it's simple – he is hurting me. But in addition to the pain, maybe even more important than the pain, is the fact that he does not care that he is hurting me. He does not care that I am unhappy, not really. My happiness is not relevant.

"Sonja, for many women sex can be uncomfortable at first. I understand. You should not feel that there is something wrong with you if sex is not the most pleasant thing for a while."

"'Not the most pleasant thing'? Were you listening to what I said, Alice?"

"I was listening. I'm not a doctor, but I've worked with hundreds of couples who have experienced similar problems. I recognize the pattern."

"The pattern?"

"There are more and more un-Christian things out there to distract us, to tempt us. We are Christian women, Sonja. The world fills our head with all of these phony ideas of false freedom. These women's magazines—if you read them you'd think that we should all have careers, the best clothes, all the ..."

"Does Adam pound on you, finish his business and then just ignore you? Does he make you bleed? Does he lie through his teeth about what he does to make himself look good, like he is in the right?"

"See what I mean? Drama, exaggeration, she is ...'

"Sonja, sex is a duty we owe our husband. Yes, we can enjoy it, but enjoy it or not, it is our duty. We must bear children. God is clear on that."

"Do you enjoy sex, Alice?"

"Not in the same way Adam does, no."

"Does Adam hurt you?"

"No, of course not."

"I'm sorry if I hurt you, Sonja. I didn't mean to. If you were... what can I do to help you like me more? Aren't you attracted to me?"

"Walter, for God's sake. Stop putting on a show for these people. Do you want some help or not?"

"We are trying to help you, Sonja. That's why we are here," Pastor offers.

"Wait a minute. Pastor, did you and Alice talk with Walter about our marriage before tonight?"

"Yes, for a few hours in Pastor Walker's office. We wanted to learn all we could, get the background in depth that helps us to be..."

"So what Walter says is Gospel. What I say means nothing."

"You see, Pastor? This is what I have to deal with, day in and day out."

"Sonja, let us help. You're just confused, that's all. Walter loves you and he wants to make you happy."

"Alice, you seem like a very nice woman, so please don't take this the wrong way. Please leave. Right now."

"Sonja, we should listen to what they have to ..."

"Walter, I'm right on the edge. You've lied to these people about what happens between us in private. There just isn't much more I can say. But, please. Stay and talk with your friends. I'll leave."

"Sonja, you can't run away from your problems," Pastor Adam warns. "You're right about that," I agree.

"Headed back to Sandy's house?" Walter asks, sarcastically.

"At least there I'll be with someone who loves me and won't hurt me. Oh, and she also never lies to me. You're a liar, Walter. That is so sad."

I know what Walter would like to do right now. He wants to jump up and threaten me and yell. But I also know that he won't because the Hunts are here.

My leaving only makes his story more credible to the Hunts and everyone else, I suppose.

The sad thing is I just don't care.

I've reached done.

I can't go through life living like this anymore.

CHAPTER FORTY

"We would love to have you back. Miss Roberts' mother was taken ill and she was called home unexpectedly to Pensacola. I was all set to put this job posting in the classifieds." Mr. Larsen hands me the ad for, "Receptionist – Barnett Bank".

"Please tear it up Mrs. Barker and come back to work on Monday morning."

"I will. Thank you so much. It means, well, it means everything to me right now."

"Are you alright, Mrs. Barker?"

"Will you call me Sonja please, Mr. Larsen?"

"Sure. What I mean is you look a little pale, tired maybe."

"I'll be ready for work next week."

"I'm sure you will Sonja. I'm just concerned for you."

I'd forgotten that Mr. Larsen is a very pleasant man. It will be nice to work for him again.

"Thanks, I'll be okay. I'm just going through some changes."

"Feel free to ask if there is anything I can do for you."

"I will. God bless you."

"Take care." Mr. Larsen answers his phone as I leave.

I walked into the bank as an unemployed young woman; a soon to be a divorced, unemployed young woman.

I walk out with a decent job in a place I like. Maybe God is looking out for me after all.

Walter wants to take me to the movies tonight.

He still holds out hope that I will give in to his pressure and manipulation and turn my body back over to him.

That is not going to happen.

God gave this body to me, not to him.

The question now is, when and how do I tell him?

When I do tell him I have to be gone, along with everything I want to take with me from the house.

I really do not want anything other than my clothes, pictures and personal items.

I damn sure do not want alimony or furniture or anything else that is his or the Barkers.

I want my freedom.

I want to live in peace and, Lord willing, repair my broken heart and someday marry a man who will love and appreciate me, who will treat me like I deserve to be treated.

I pray for guidance and I pray for strength. I pray for Walter.

"You look nice, honey."

"Thanks, Walter."

"Did you enjoy the movie?"

"Sure. I like all of Hitchcocks' films."

"They're too dark for me. Someone always gets killed or goes to prison, or both. Sonja, before I forget I need you to do a favor for me on Monday. My car is acting up, I scheduled a repair time with the …"

"Walter, I'm sorry. I can't do any favors for you on Monday."

"Why not?"

"Well, I was going to tell you tomorrow, but I guess now is as good as time as any. I'm going back to work at the bank."

"What?"

"I'm going back to work at Barnett Bank in my old job, as a receptionist."

"You didn't say a word to me about this, I don't understand. Don't I give you enough money, Sonja? Aren't you …"

"The money is not the issue; well, it is in a way. Yes, you give me enough money, Walter. But I need my own money, my own income."

"Sonja, I just don't understand."

"Walter, let's go home. We need to talk. The car is not the place to do it."

"What's wrong with you?"

"Nothing is wrong with me, Walter. I'm sorry to tell you that. You seem convinced that I need help of some kind, but I don't need any help."

"I'm the one who needs help."

"Yes, Walter. You don't want to see it."

"Oh, I 'see it' alright. I see everything *very* clearly."

"I wish that were true. I've prayed for that so many times."

"We need to talk."

"Yes, Walter."

He turns left on to a side street and pulls the car off to the side of the road. "How about here, can we talk here?"

"I want a divorce, Walter."

"A divorce? You've got to be …"

"I want a divorce. I've tried everything I know to save this marriage. You won't listen to me, you won't listen to reason."

"You would break our sacred vows? You promised to …"

"And you promised to 'love and cherish me', Walter. Who broke the vows first? You did."

"This friend of yours, she is …"

"Stop it. Sandy has nothing to do with this, nothing at all. I make up my own mind about things. Quit blaming other people for your problems."

"So, you gotta job, you want a divorce. What's his name?"

"Whose name?"

"Your boyfriend's name?"

"That is…I'm done. Take me home. Now."

"Never give me orders. You don't tell me what to do."

"Then I'll drive myself," I say, as I reach for the keys. I don't get them, but I do knock them to the floor.

Walter quickly scoops them up, opens his door and gets out of the car.

I open my door, get out and say, "Give me the keys, Walter. I'm going home."

"You want these? Come and get 'em."

"Walter, I'm through playing games with you."

"You're through when I say you're through."

"Give me the keys."

"Oh, so you do want to play, do ya?"

Walter grabs me and rips my blouse, almost pulling it off. "Stop it! Don't touch me!"

He shoves me down, I land on my back. The back of my head hits the concrete.

I'm dazed for a minute.

Walter rips my skirt off me.

I'm lying there on the side of the road with only my bra and panties on.

"Take off the rest and I'm sure you'll be able to get a ride home you miserable whore," Walter says as he gets back in the car and drives away.

CHAPTER FORTY ONE

He's gone!

I don't believe it. Walter left me here stranded on the side of road in my underwear.

He took my clothes too, I notice. I don't even have my ripped blouse to use to cover myself.

I see headlights approaching. I scramble behind a bush as the car passes.

Am I more angry or frightened? Hard to say. I feel both emotions in equal intensity.

Walter called me a "whore". That's exactly what he wants me to be. Maybe when I leave him he will find himself a good whore and pay for her services by the hour.

The main road is only a few yards away.

I look around. I see the lights on in a house on the other side of the street. Should I knock on the door?

How would they react to a girl in her underwear begging for help? I can't stay out here all night.

My head hurts. I banged it pretty hard on the ground. I'm not bleeding though, thank God.

More headlights are coming. A car is slowing down. It's Walter.

He stops the car, rolls down the passenger side window and says, "Get in."

Getting back in the car is the last thing I want to do; well, it is the second to last thing I want to do. The last thing I want to do is spend another second out here in my underwear.

I don't say a word, but I do get back in. My ripped clothes are on the seat.

I put my blouse on, but my skirt is torn to shreds.

From the direction Walter is headed, I assume that he is taking us home. "Did you have some time to think?" Walter asks.

"Time to think? Are you ser…"

"To reconsider what you said to me."

"Walter, just take me home."

"And then what?"

"What do you mean and then what? Walter, my God."

"I need you , Sonja. I need my wife back."

"It's too late for that, Walter. It's been too late for a while now. You just left me by the side of the road in my …"

"Shut up," Walter says, in a very menacing tone. I'm scared now, really scared.

What will he do next? Inside part of me 'switches gears'. I need to think differently.

For ten minutes we sit next to each other in complete silence. This makes me even more frightened.

I know that my car is waiting for me back home. My purse is right where I left it under the car seat and I know where fifty dollars in emergency money is hidden in the kitchen.

As we pull into the driveway all I want to do is get to safety. This house is not safety.

This is Walter's house. It's not mine any longer. Walter gets out, as do I. I have my purse in one hand, my ripped skirt in the other. We walk towards the house and stop on the front porch.

"Let me tell you how it's gonna be, woman." Walter says. "I take what's mine whenever I want to."

He grabs me and shoves me down.

I turn and slap him.

He hits me very hard. I'm not sure what's really happening for a second or two. But then I am sure.

Walter has me bent over the edge of our porch and he is humping me like a crazed lunatic.

I'm being raped in my own front yard.

Thank God the porch and house lights are off. Maybe no one will see.

But maybe someone should see.

Walter is so excited it only takes him a minute to finish.

He stands up, pulls up his pants, walks back to his car and drives away. I sink down below the front porch wall, curl up in a ball and start to cry.

CHAPTER FORTY TWO

"Mom, we need to talk."

"Can't we talk at church tomorrow, Sonja? Vince isn't feeling well, I need to …"

"I'm not going to church tomorrow."

"Why not? What's happened?"

"Walter attacked me. He hit me, bent me over the front porch rail and raped me."

"What did you say?"

"You heard me, mother."

"My God? Where are you?"

"At the house, by myself. Walter took off and I don't want to be around when he comes back. I'm scared, mom. Really, really scared."

"Come over here. Right now."

"You can't tell Dad, not yet."

"You can tell him yourself, in your time, your way."

"I'm leaving now."

"Try and stay calm, honey. Just come home."

As soon as I see her I start to cry. Mom is completely beside herself.

We sit for a few minutes, hugging and crying. Then I tell her the whole story.

"What are you goin' to do, honey? You have to face Walter sooner or later."

"I know. He's probably cooked up one hell of a lie by now. I'm the villain, no doubt."

"You understand how serious this is, don't you, Sonja?"

"I understood how serious it was when I was being raped in my own front yard."

"Sonja, quit talking like that. Never speak of such things to anyone but family."

"Why not? That's what he did to me."

"I'm tellin' ya, don't say such things to people. No one wants to hear it."

"He could have killed me, mother."

"Sonja, I don't think Walter would have killed you."

"You don't believe me, do you."

"Of course I believe you, dear."

"You think I'm making it sound worse than it really was."

"Sonja, I know you're unhappy. You're not the first girl to marry the wrong guy.

A divorce isn't the worst thing in the world, if you end up getting …"

"If I end up getting a divorce? Unreal, mom. Walter is a sick person. He needs help… no. He should be locked up."

"Sonja, you don't really mean that, honey."

"I don't?"

We both react as we hear the front door open and close.

My father is home. As usual, he spent his Saturday night working at a second job. "What we got here?" Father says, as he walks in the kitchen and sees mother and I huddled together and crying.

"Your daughter had a rough night."

"That so?"

"I'm divorcing Walter, Dad."

"What kinda foolish talk is that? You two have a fight or somethin'?"

"He raped me. Right out in the open for the entire world to see."

"Whoa now. Slow down, missy. Walter wouldn't go doin' nothin' like that."

"I just told you …"

"I heard what ya said, Sonja." Dad puts down his bag and walks over to the fridge.

"Dad," I scream, or try to scream through my tears, "Walter hit me and he raped me!"

"Now don't go gettin' all hysterical."

"You don't care. You're just like him!" When I say this I lose control and collapse into my mother's arms.

"Lord have mercy! Faye, ya need to deal with this craziness. It's too much for me."

My Father picks up his glass of tea and leftover half a sandwich, walks into the den and switches on the tv.

On the worst night of my life, when I'm crying out in agony and in desperate need of love, all my blessed father can do is dismiss me and walk away.

I think…no, I know.

My father's indifference towards my suffering hurts far more than being raped. Mother sees how hurt I am but she says nothing to her husband.

"Let's get you to bed, hon," is all she says.

I'm too tired to do anything other than collapse.

I have not cleaned up Walter's mess between my legs. As disgusting as that is to me, all my energy is gone.

Somewhere, deep inside my soul, a Voice softly speaks to me.

He tells me that He loves me, that I will survive this trial and that He is always near.

God's love, His mercy is sufficient for us. Preachers have been telling me that all my life. I finally know what it means.

CHAPTER FORTY THREE

"Do you have everything?"

"That's it."

"You don't want anything else?"

"No, I just never want to see him again, for as long as I live."

"That's not going to happen, you know that."

"I need to leave him a note, my wedding ring and the house key."

"Dearest Walter," I write. "If you ever touch me again, I'll kill you."

"Nice," Sandy compliments.

"I mean it."

"I don't doubt it."

We finish gathering up my clothes and other personal items. How lucky we are that Walter went to work this morning; luckier still that Mr. Larsen let me report for work on Tuesday rather than today.

"Bart, how can I thank you? Having you here is, well, it's nice to know that I'm safe."

"I don't know exactly what happened between you and Walter, but I know it had to be serious or you wouldn't be doing this," Bart says.

"Are you sure you don't mind if Sandy and I live together for a while in your guest house?"

"Not at all. I'm lending you Ralphie as well."

"Who is Ralphie?"

"He's their German Shepherd," Sandy answers. "He doesn't like strangers.

Makes a lot of noise when someone he doesn't know is on the property." Everything I own is in the back of Bart Scott's station wagon.

Sandy holds my hand.

No more husband, but now I have a roommate. And a dog.

Things are definitely looking up.

"Sonja, you have a visitor," Mr. Larsen says as I finish the filing he asked me to do.

"Oh?"

"It's your husband, I think."

"Oh."

I was expecting this to happen sooner or later. It was inevitable.

For the past three days I have been peeking around every corner, choosing where I parked very carefully, staying in public places, remaining visible and never alone.

Poor Ralphie has had to sleep on the front porch. Not because he was bad, but because we needed him to guard the front door.

"Mr. Larsen, can I use the spare office, the one up front?"

"Of course. There is a phone on the desk. If you feel in the least bit uncomfortable, just pick up the receiver and dial one. I'll come running."

"Thank you. I'm very sorry that I have to…"

"Don't worry about that, Sonja. Handle your business."

Thank God for Mr. Larsen. I told him that Walter had been rough with me and that I was filing for a divorce. More than that he didn't need, or want, to know.

"Sonja."

"Walter."

"I would like to talk with you."

"Okay, we can …"

"How about dinner?"

"Walter, if you want to talk with me it's in this office, right now, or it's never."

Walter doesn't react, although I know on the inside he is seething.

We sit down and close the door. The window faces the lobby; everyone in the bank can see, but not hear, us.

"Sonja, I'm sorry about what happened. I just wasn't …"

"I have found a lawyer who will handle our divorce for a reasonable price. It will take me a while to get the papers drawn up. I don't want any…"

"Slow down, Sonja. I know you're steamed at me, but pl …"

"Steamed? You think I'm 'steamed' at you?"

"You have a right to be."

"I'm divorcing you. You better get used to the idea."

"The Hunts have agreed to…"

"You told them what, Walter? What lie did you tell them?"

"I didn't tell them any …"

"Did you tell them that you hit me? That you raped me in my own front yard?"

"I never raped you. What are you talking about?"

"I'm…I'm just done, Walter. You don't want to even try to get it."

"Let's take this to the Lord, together. Pastor Walker and the Hunts will …"

"I have already taken it to the Lord."

"Sonja, I know that you're a Christian woman. You don't want a divorce."

"Enough. I may be young, but I'm sure not stupid. It's time for you to leave."

"I love you, Sonja. You're my wife. I need you to come home."

"Stay away from me. Don't bother me at Bart's house, either. This is your first and last warning."

"Don't you threaten me, Sonja."

I pick up the phone and get ready to dial one. Walter isn't stupid either, he knows what's up. "I'm leaving, no need for a scene."

I put the phone back in the cradle.

"This isn't over. Not by a longshot. I will not stand for you divorcing me, no way."

"Good bye."

Walter leaves in a huff. Mr. Larsen nods at me. I go back to work.

I pray a short prayer asking God to protect me, to keep me safe from my husband. I'll need His protection because I believe Walter.

This isn't over. Not by a longshot.

CHAPTER FORTY FOUR

"Even if I got down on one knee?" Sandy begs. "Not even then," I say, laughing.

"God this lasagna is great! Everything you cook is fantastic. You're all I could hope for in a spouse."

"All beauty, no brains, but I can cook."

"Perfect combination."

"Hey, don't give him any more of that!" I shout, as I see Sandy slipping Raphie another bite of table food.

"Why not?"

"Did you look in the back room? That'll tell you why not."

"Yuck."

"Yea yuck. A huge mess."

"You clean up dog messes too? The perfect wife."

"Soon to be ex-wife."

"I was going to ask you about that."

"It takes a bit to get it all done, but at least he's been served with papers."

"How much did it cost?"

"Around two hundred bucks."

"I guess that's one thing I should be grateful for. Mine cost me nothing."

"Best money I ever spent."

"I told you that your Grandmother called, didn't I?"

"We spoke on my break at work."

"What a sweet lady. I fell in love with her over the phone."

"She's the best. I need to go see her."

"You've always been close to your grandparents?"

"Forever."

"Oh, she sent you a letter too. It's over on the end table."

"She told me it was coming."

I retrieve the letter and open it as Ralphie puts his head on my lap. I already know what's in it.

"I have an aunt in Atlanta."

"Yea?" Sandy says as she clears the table. Ever since we moved in together we had a deal. I cook and she cleans up. We both think we're getting the best part of the bargain.

"Your mom's sister?"

"No, my father's sister."

"Hope to hell she's nothing like him."

"Me too. I've never met her. The only thing I know is her name. Grace Bowen."

"Another Sonja story. Let me make some tea and you can tell me all about it."

I've been living with Sandy for almost two months now. While my life has been turned upside down, I've never been happier. I live with a nice person, a "normal" person, whatever the heck that is, I suppose. Normal to me means pleasant and kind. We have become as close as sisters in a very short time.

"My Grandma had a child out of wedlock before she married Lester. She gave the girl up for adoption. I guess when you do that you don't normally get know what happens to the child, who her parents are, where she lives, all that."

"It depends. Years ago they did things differently. There were fewer rules."

"Anyway, Grandma kept this all a big secret. She told Grandpa everything but that was it, no one else. She told me about Grace when I visited her, you remember, when she broke her leg? Somehow she was able to keep track of her over the years. I guess my visit got her to thinking and now, well, she wants me to go see my aunt."

"You gonna go?"

"No *we're* gonna go."

"I'd be thrilled."

"What do you think? Should we just show up at her door and say hi, I'm your long lost niece? Should we call first?"

"What do you know about her?"

"Well," I say, as I pick up the letter and start to read it, "Grace is school teacher. Elementary school. She has three kids."

"New cousins."

"Her husband's name is Arthur Bowen. Doctor Arthur Bowen. He's a surgeon."

"Big money then. They're rich."

"Suppose so. Sandy, what if . ."

"What if what?"

"Why would someone like Grace Bowen want to know someone like me? Maybe Grandma is wrong. Maybe we should just leave well enough alone."

"Blood is blood. You want to meet her, what makes you think that she doesn't feel the same?"

"Do I have to tell her about her brother?"

"Yea, I suppose so. She has a right to know."

"Lord in heaven I was afraid you'd say that."

We laugh and finish putting away the dinner dishes. "Ever been to Atlanta?" I ask.

"A few times. I love the city."

"Me too. I always kinda wanted to live there."

"Who knows what the future holds." Sandy pauses, sniffs and says, "What is that smell?"

Ralphie walks into the kitchen with his tail between his legs and sits by the back door.

Sandy looks at me and reaches for the bucket and the rags. She tries to hand me the cleaning supplies.

"Un uh sister. You fed him the lasagna."

"Meanie."

CHAPTER FORTY FIVE

My mother is very upset. She never calls me past ten pm unless something is really wrong.

"Slow down, Mom. Tell me again what you know."

"He's gone. He left a note saying that he wouldn't be back."

"When was the last time that you saw Luke?"

"Three days ago. I found the note this morning."

"Did he say why he left?"

This is a stupid question, we both know why he left, but I ask anyway. "He said that he couldn't live in his father's house one more day."

"What do you want me to say?"

"I want you to find your brother and bring him back home."

"I have no way...wait a minute. If you think. I do not know where he is."

"Would you tell me if you did?"

I pause. I'm really not sure what my honest response is to this question. "I don't know."

"Sonja, please just…"

"I will tell you this. As of right now I have no idea where Luke is or what he is doing." This is true. Luke said not one word to me about running away from home.

"I just don't understand, what could he be…

"What do you not understand?"

"We gave Luke a good home, clothes, safety, a proper…

"Father is a cold hearted man. Luke was never good enough for him. You understand, you just don't want to face the truth."

"Sonja, just because you're all 'grown-up' and getting a divorce does not mean that you have the…"

"Fine, I'll keep my opinions to myself."

"Vince could really use some time with his sister right now." I agree. Vince does need me and I need him.

For the past three months I have been avoiding any contact with my father.

Mom and I have met for lunch a few times and we talk on the phone but I have not been back to the house.

I don't know what I will say to my father when we meet again, face to face.

Part of me just wants to bury the whole thing, take my mother's "ostrich" approach and pretend that it never happened.

But I can't pretend. I'm done with living like that, it's not healthy. It's not Christian.

What is Christian is forgiveness.

I remember once a visiting pastor came and spoke at our church. He was from Arkansas. His topic was forgiveness. The truth is, more often than I should, I drift off during the preaching. But I remember this particular preacher and this sermon vividly.

He said that forgiveness is a gift we give ourselves. We don't give another forgiveness because they deserve it or to make them feel better, we do it to heal our own soul. To "dump our trash off in the garbage can and move on". Those were his exact words.

I have a lot of trash to drop off.

What I need is a really big, empty garbage can.

"I want to see Vince."

"Our door is always open, honey."

"Why don't we start by me taking him for the weekend. Sandy won't mind, she likes him."

"Thank you, Sonja. I'm sorry, too. I know that you think I'm a lousy mother, but..."

"You are not a lousy mother. I love you very much."

"But?"

"You know what I think, I don't need to say it again."

"Maybe you'll do better."

"Love you, Mom."

"Love you too, honey. Bye." I'm already doing better.

I tried my best with my husband.

When I could see that I was fighting an impossible battle, I refused to sacrifice my soul on the altar of a selfish, angry man.

Mother made a different choice. She makes that same choice every single day, over and over again.

Luke leaving home is a result of that choice.

There is simply no getting around it, or sugar coating it. But there is forgiveness.

CHAPTER FORTY SIX

"I like your car," Sandy says.
"It is the one possession I kept from my marriage."
"I'm surprised Walter didn't try and take it."
"He got off easy in the financial department."
"How soon will you be Sonja Kent again?"
"Still not sure about that... hey, were we supposed to go that way?"
"Oh gosh. I think so. That sign said 'Doraville', didn't it." I pull over and wait for the traffic to clear to make a U turn.
"It's a good thing I like redheads or I'd fire you. You're a lousy navigator."
"True enough, but I'm cute and I'm great company."
"Do you think we should have called? I mean we are just dropping in on a Saturday. What if ..."
"Stop it. We're almost there. Have a little faith."
"Speaking of faith, I wanted to tell you that I like your church."
"Reverend was sure glad you could play for us last Sunday. I think, no, I know that he wants you to take over the job full time."
"I might just do that."
"Sonja Kent a Presbyterian huh? You're movin' up in the world."

"Do you think Grace goes to church? I wonder if she has any ..."

"You're very nervous."

"Wouldn't you be?"

"I guess. She's the lucky one to be meeting you. I'll be sure to tell her what a really great lady you are."

"Okay, you're not fired."

"Do you want to hear more about Doraville?"

"Sure."

"You know I made a special trip down to the library just to get this article for you."

"Now if I could only get you to fold your laundry."

"Doraville, Georgia. GM built a car factory there a few years ago and the place boomed. Went from a sleepy little farm town to an important place overnight."

"I'll bet Dr. Bowen works at the hospital."

"They've got one, it's brand new."

"How close are they to Atlanta?"

"The city is a few miles away. It says here more and more people are starting to drive from Doraville to Atlanta and back every day for work. Live in the country, work in the city."

"I shouldn't have worn this blue dress. I mean look at me, I'm all wrinkled."

"You look fine, sugar."

"Do you think she'll like me? I mean for real, no kidding around?"

"Stop worrying. We're almost there."

We pull up to the house. My stomach is tied in knots.

A thought pops into my head. Ronnie Cantwell is watching me.

I know that he has been dead for over ten years. I never met the man. His picture is in the envelope in my hand.

It is a picture of Mary and Ronnie together, arm in arm, at the old Augusta dance hall.

Taken more than forty five years ago, it is faded and the edges are frayed.

The woman inside this house has no idea that a stranger is about to show her a picture of her parents.

"Are we just gonna sit here?" Sandy asks.

"First, we pray."

Sandy is like me, we don't normally pray in public or with someone else unless it's Sunday and we are in church.

"Lord, let me do the right thing and say the right words. I do not want to hurt this person. Give me strength, Jesus," I pray.

"Sonja, just be yourself. This will be a good day I promise." Sandy gives me a kiss on the cheek and we get out of the car. "My gosh, what a place," Sandy says.

"Yea, wow."

The house isn't a mansion, but it's very big and looks brand new. There are two cars in the driveway, a Cadillac and a Chevy. The Chevy still has the "new car" sticker in the back window. The lawns are perfectly manicured; the landscaping was obviously done by professionals.

We hear water splashing and look to our right. Behind a small barrier fence we see a water fountain, done in brick. The patio is slightly offset from the house and looks like a picture from *Home and Gardens* magazine.

I can hear children playing in the back yard. This encourages me. If kids are here Grace is probably home.

I ring the bell. A man answers. "Morning young ladies."

"Good morning," we answer.

"Are you girls selling something? Going door to door?"

"No," we say, almost in unison.

"Well then, how can I help you?"

"Are you Dr. Bowen, Dr. Arthur Bowen?"

"Yes. Do I know you girls?"

"No," I answer. "Is your wife named Grace?"

"Yes."

"I came by today to speak with her. Is she home?"

"She is. Grace is in the kitchen. May I tell her what this is regarding?"

"Doctor Bowen," I say, "I don't mean to be rude, but I think I should say what I have to say to Grace first. That would be the proper thing to do."

"By all means," Dr. Bowen says, "welcome to our home."

CHAPTER FORTY SEVEN

My soon to be former in-laws are wealthy people and they have a very nice home. That said, it doesn't hold a candle to this place.

I've never seen anything like it. Although not asked to, I want to take my shoes off. I'm afraid to get a speck of dust on anything.

It reminds me of Miss Bloom's home, only with a lot more expensive furniture in every room. Whoever keeps this house is meticulous and has great taste. I'm assuming that person is Grace.

Dr. Bowen leads us into the kitchen as he calls out his wife's name. I grab Sandy's arm when I see her.

It's uncanny. I'm looking at my grandmother forty five years younger. They're not twins, but the resemblance is nothing short of remarkable.

One thing is for sure, as soon as Grace takes a look at the picture she will have no doubt that I am telling her the truth.

"Honey, this...you know what, I forgot to ask your names."

"Sonja Kent," I say.

"Sandy Combs."

"Sonja said that she would like to speak with you, dear."

"Hi girls," Grace says. "I'm busy as heck preparing tonight's meal, but please come in and sit down."

"Having a party?" I ask.

"My daughter's tenth birthday party. I'm expecting forty kids and their parents."

"Oh my!" Dr. Bowen says. "I completely forgot. I have to cover for Steve. I'll be back by five dear."

Dr. Bowen kisses his wife and hurries away.

Grace puts a pan of rolls in the oven, washes her hands and sits down at the table with us.

She is a beautiful woman. Classy, that's the term that comes to mind. Grace is elegant. Just like Grace Kelly I think, maybe …

"Sonja, is it? You wanted to talk with me about something?" I realize that I've been staring at Grace without saying a word. "Mrs. Bowen," I begin. "I came by …"

"It's Grace, dear. My mother-in-law is Mrs. Bowen."

"Grace, I have something to tell you."

"Good news, I hope." I hope so too.

"I know that you were adopted, Grace. Your father owned a clothing store in Atlanta. Your mom stayed home with you and your brother. You teach elementary school at Oakcliff. I've been told all about you."

"I guess so. Who told you about me?"

"Your mother."

"Someone has been playing with you, dear. My mother died ten years ago."

"Your mother is alive and well and lives in Augusta."

Grace didn't get it at first. A few seconds went by before she realized what I said and what it meant.

"Sonja, who are you?"

"I'm your niece."

"I…" Grace didn't know what to say.

"I brought this picture to show you." I hand Grace the picture. "They are your birth parents, Ronnie Cantwell and Mary Kent. Grandma might have been pregnant with you when this photo was taken."

Grace looks at the photo. Then she looks at me. She starts to cry.

Oh Lord, I knew it! a voice screams in my head. I had no right to come here, to upset this very nice lady, to...

"Sonja, thank you. I always wondered... I spent years trying to..." Grace couldn't speak through her tears.

"It's okay that I told you? You wanted to know?"

"Heavens yes!" Grace says in a loud voice. "You are answered prayer." We give each other a big hug.

"Are we related too?" Grace asks, looking at Sandy. "No, I'm not that lucky. I'm Sonja's roommate."

"No you're not. You're my best friend."

"Sonja, honey, I want to talk with you for hours. I have so many questions..." Grace stopped. A buzzer went off. It was time to tend to something on the stove.

"You picked a busy day to tell me all this honey."

"Can we help?"

"Can you cook?"

"Can she cook? I eat like a queen. Sonja knows her way around a kitchen."

"How about you?"

"Nah, not me. But I'm a great dishwasher."

"I need you both then. Can you girls stay for the day?"

Would you consider adopting me? I think. I never want to leave this wonderful home.

"We have no plans."

"Now you do."

CHAPTER FORTY EIGHT

"When did he get home?" I ask, switching the receiver to my left ear.

"This morning before we left for church. The police brought him back. He made it all the way to the Alabama border hitchhiking. If your father hadn't alerted the police he might have just kept going. I never would have ..."

"Mother, it's okay. I hope Dad didn't beat him or anything."

"No, he didn't," Mom said, with a sense of resolve. "I made sure he didn't."

Good for you ma, I say in my mind. About damn time. "Are you free for lunch tomorrow?"

"I'd love to have lunch with you, honey."

"We need to talk about something."

"Please, no more bad news, Sonja."

"How about some absolutely wonderful news?"

"I could sure use some. Did you and Sandy have fun in Atlanta?"

"I'll tell you all about it tomorrow."

I'm ready to hang up the phone when mother says, "Got something else to tell you. Probably shouldn't wait 'til lunch."

"Okay."

"Walter is not going to sign your divorce papers."

"What?"

"After church today he told us, I guess he knew we'd tell you, that he is not going to sign the papers."

"I don't understand."

"He wants you back, honey. He made that clear too."

"That will never happen."

"That's what he said about signing your papers."

"We'll see about that."

"He wants to know who you're seeing."

"Who I'm seeing?"

"Your boyfriend's name."

"I don't have a boyfriend, mother. You know that."

"Walter don't know that."

"Yes he does. And even if I did, it wouldn't be any of his business anyway."

"It ain't gonna be easy, hon. Walter is very determined."

"I gotta go, mom. Usual place at noon?"

"See ya then, honey."

My lawyer warned me this could happen. I guess the law says I can't force Walter to sign anything and without his consent I can't divorce him.

But I refuse to let Walter's nonsense dampen my spirits. I have a new aunt and uncle.

I did not want to leave Doraville.

Neither did Sandy. The Bowens fell in love with her too.

My cousins are sweet kids and Doreen, their oldest, is only two years younger than me.

I can't wait to tell mother all about them.

But as I hang up the phone I know that there is someone else I need to talk to right now.

I dial Grandma Mary's phone. She answers. "Hi Grandma."

"Hello dear."

I had not told Grandma that I was going to see Grace this weekend. I didn't want to build her hopes up or cause her to worry.

"I went to see Grace."

In the background I can hear Grandma pull out a chair in the kitchen and sit down.

"What happened?"

"You have a wonderful daughter. She is the sweetest person, just the best. Sandy and I just showed up unannounced at her door and we ended up staying with her for the whole weekend. We got to know her kids, her husband, we…"

While I was carrying on, Grandma was weeping. I knew they were tears of joy. "What's she like, Sonja?"

"She looks like you. She's smart, funny and I think she is very happily married."

"I bet she hates me."

"Not at all. She spent a couple of thousand dollars over the years trying to find out who you were. Grace even hired a private detective, but she got nowhere."

"Did you take pictures?"

"Lots."

"Oh honey, I'd love to see 'em. It would mean a lot."

"She wants to meet you."

"I…I…are ya sure?"

"How's next weekend sound? I'll drive back up to Doraville on Friday after work, pick up Grace and we will be there Saturday morning."

"Honey, that's awfully expensive for you. Let me send you some money for .."

"Don't worry about a thing. Grace is paying for everything. The Bowens are quite well off."

"Hard to believe. After all these years. I suppose she'll be real disappointed that her mother is some backwoods hick."

"Grace isn't like that at all. You'll see."

"Ya know I had the strangest feelin' last Friday. I was in the kitchen makin' Lester a meal when I could swear…I must be goin' batty in my old age."

"What Grandma?"

"I could swear that Ronnie was standing in the room with me. I couldn't see him or anythin', just feel him."

"About what time was that? When you felt Ronnie was near to you?"

"Supper time or so, I guess. Six o'clock maybe."

A chill runs up my spine.

It was exactly six o'clock on Friday when Sandy and I pulled up to Grace's house.

CHAPTER FORTY NINE

"Pastor Walker would like to meet with you, meet with both of us," Walter says.

"No thanks. God bless him though. Please tell him that I said hello."

"We still haven't found a new piano player. Miss Hicks tries her best, but she isn't that talented."

"Good luck," I say and sincerely mean. I have no ill will towards my former church.

"Why do we have to meet here, at the bank? Couldn't I buy you lunch or coffee?"

"What you could do is sign the divorce papers."

"Sonja, I've given you some time to cool down, to reconsider things. Why are you still interested in pursuing a divorce?"

I sigh and look around the bank. Everything is decorated for the holidays. We have a huge Christmas tree in the lobby, wreaths and garland everywhere and the tellers are all wearing Santa hats. With only two weeks to go before Christmas everyone is in a festive mood.

But rather than being happy and light-hearted, I am sitting here in this empty office with Walter trying to resolve that which should already be resolved. Trying to talk some sense into a fool.

I'd probably do better talking to the wall.

"Walter I don't how I can be more plain with you. Our marriage is over."

"You could at least have the decency to tell me his name."

"There is no one else, Walter. I am not dating."

"Why lie, Sonja?"

"Walter, don't…please, just sign the papers. Don't you want to start over? Find a new wife?" As I say this I pray, dear God when Walter re-marries let him treat her well, not like he treated me.

"God gave me a wife. We swore to God we would stay together until death do us part. Have you forgotten that?"

This is getting real silly now, I tell myself.

"Walter, you raped me in our front yard. You called me a whore. You treated me like a slave. Please, just sign the divorce papers. It's over."

"No!" Walter shouts and pounds his fist on the desk.

This startles me and I jump. Mr. Larsen hears the fist slam too and he looks over at me. I wave at him and signal that I'm okay.

"That guy?" Walter asks.

"Grow up, Walter. That's my boss."

"Always wondered how you got this job."

"Okay," I say. My patience is at an end. "If you refuse to sign the divorce papers then we have nothing else to talk about. It's time for you to go."

"You like this, don't ya, being able to order me around in your little bank. God is watching you, Sonja. You can treat me poorly but He sees. You can't hide from God."

"I don't have to hide from God, Walter. But rapists do."

I can see the anger well up in him. Walter's eyes give away his every mood. He wants to hit me, I can tell. But he can't in here, thank God.

"This isn't over. We are not over."

I'm done talking. All I want is for Walter to leave.

Walter stands, walks to the door and then stops. He turns and says, "You have a duty to your husband. You will perform your duty."

Walter opens the door and then slams it shut.

I know exactly what he meant by his statement. He is going to try and rape me again.

Since we are still legally married I don't think I could press charges for rape if he attacks me. He knows this too. Walter is many things, stupid isn't one of them.

Now I'm just angry. Not scared or hurt or anything but furious.

I vow to God that Walter will never touch me again.

No matter what, I will not submit to one more humping from Walter Barker.

CHAPTER FIFTY

"I'm so nervous," Grace admits.

"I know exactly how you feel. Not long ago I was in your shoes."

"It's hard to describe, Sonja. What it's like to be adopted."

We are driving through a thick forest on our way to Augusta. We decided it would be better if I drove so Aunt Grace could relax and think about things.

"Do you know how many times I wished that ..." I stop myself. Badmouthing my father is not something I want to do. "What do you wish, Sonja?"

"Oh, nothing. Family is tough, that's all."

"My parents told me that I was adopted when I was eight years old. At first it didn't really mean anything to me. Nothing changed in my life, of course. I wish you could have met them, Sonja. My parents were the best."

"I wish I could have too."

"But as I got older I started to wonder, why did my parents give me up? I mean, didn't they love me? Was my mother was dead? Were both my birth parents dead? For a year or two I really fretted over all this, it made me feel bad about myself."

"It must have been a rough time for you."

"When I was seventeen... that was a long time ago, dear," Sonja says, smiling as she squeezes my hand. "A girlfriend of mine got pregnant. She was scared to death. Back then it was even worse than it is now, all of the secrecy and shame. Anyway this frightened child, Milly, she came to me begging for forty dollars. She figured that because my folks owned a clothing store I was rich and probably had forty dollars lying around."

"What did she want forty dollars for?"

"An abortion."

"Oh my." I was beginning to understand where Grace was going with all this.

"I didn't give her the money, although I did have forty dollars saved. Back in those days forty dollars was a huge sum."

"What happened to Millie?"

"She went to some ten dollar back door abortionist and disposed of the baby. In the process she got an infection and she died too, a week later."

"Lord have mercy!" Now I squeeze Grace's hand. I look over at my aunt. She's crying.

"I still haven't forgiven myself for not helping Millie. I should have..."

"Grace, that was so long ago."

"I know dear, but life is precious. Death cannot be undone. What I should have done is taken Millie to see someone, a pastor, somebody. I should have told my parents. I could have done *something*, but I didn't."

"Why not?"

"Because when Millie said that she was pregnant and didn't want the child I saw my mother standing there. I wondered if my mother thought of disposing me in the trash like Millie was planning to do. The thought of that, killing an unborn child so callously, it really unnerved me."

"Grace, I can tell you for a fact that Grandma never, I mean never, thought of aborting you. She would not do such a thing."

"Oh my, all these memories," Grace says, wiping her eyes. "The whole tragedy taught me exactly what you just said. My mother did want me. She sacrificed and suffered and gave birth to me. I was given two great parents, a wonderful life. I wasn't mad at my birth mother anymore, I was grateful. This all sounds silly, doesn't it."

"No, not in the least bit. I don't know what it's like to be adopted, but I know all about people being cruel and selfish."

Grace leans over and kisses me on the cheek.

"You are answered prayer, hon. Answered prayer," she says.

Along the way to my Grandparent's house I tell Grace about my father and Walter in detail. She is a good listener and is very interested in what's happening in my life. I tell her about Miss Bloom, my music, how much I like to play the piano.

The closer we get to Grandma's house the more I talk. I can see that I am distracting her, which is exactly what I'm trying to do.

"Kind of hard to find this place," Grace observes.

"Pretty close to town, but still isolated. Some would say that's a good thing."

"I would be one of those 'some'."

"My best memories are here."

We pull up to the house. When I look over Grace is shaking like a leaf in the wind.

"Aunt Grace, trust me. This will be a great day." My redhead friend told me that once and boy was she right.

We get out of the car and walk up to the house. Grace takes my hand.

I feel honored. That's the only way to describe it; privileged to be alive and here and to witness this re-union.

It was a re-union. Although four decades plus had passed, these two people shared a bond that only a mother and child can share.

"Hello?" I say as we walk in the house. The door is unlocked and open, as always.

I hear nothing. Grandma knows that we are coming. She has to be here. From the kitchen I hear a small noise, like feet shuffling.

Grace and I walk into the kitchen, still holding hands.

Grandma Mary is sitting at the table. She is wearing a brand new dress, her hair is all done up and she has a bunch of flowers in her hand.

Grace looks at Mary, Mary looks at Grace. Neither of them says a word for a few seconds.

Then Mary says, "Please don't hate me, Grace. I love ya very, very much child." Grace lets go of my hand and walks over to her mother.

"I don't hate you, mother. I'm just so happy...all I ever wanted was to..." They embrace.

I'm crying harder than both of them and they are really crying.

Some people say that miracles don't happen, that people who believe in such things are foolish dreamers.

I wish those people could see what I'm seeing. Then they would know that miracles do happen. The world is full of pain and spite and meanness.

Lord knows I've endured enough of those things in my short lifetime.

But the Good Book says, "Greater is He that is in me than he who is in the world."

The devil doesn't always win.

In fact, in the end, he never does.

CHAPTER FIFTY ONE

I'm really not sure about this, but I feel that it must be done. I cannot dodge the man forever.

My mind is focused on what I'll be doing later today, which is picking up Sandy from work and driving to Doraville. We are spending the Christmas weekend with Aunt Grace and her family.

Here I am standing at the front door of my father's house. A door I swore I would never stand in front of again.

I'm thinking about last year at this time. I was so sick; the blood poisoning was beginning to take its toll on my body. Walter was still humping me night after night. It was not a pleasant Christmas.

I thank God that things are better now, that my path is becoming easier to see if not always easy to follow.

Grace wants to meet her brother. When I go inside I'll tell him that his sister would like to get to know him. Will he care? Probably not.

I need to forgive my father.

I'm still not sure quite how to do that, what is required.

Simply saying the words seems so meaningless. Anyone can say the words. The hard part is truly letting go of the pain.

I love my mother and my brothers. They live in this house. That means I have to be a part of this family again if I want them in my life.

And I do want them in my life. I need them in my life.

Lord give me strength.

"Hi, hon," Mom says as she opens the door. "Merry Christmas."

"Merry Christmas," I say and give her a hug and a kiss.

I can hear my brothers talking in the kitchen. "Is he home?"

"Just getting out of the shower."

"Don't tell me that he worked this morning."

"Triple time pay. He's going back at six o'clock." I sigh. God bless him, I say in my mind.

"Hi sis!" little Vince yells when he sees me. "Thanks so much for the train set. I set it up over here, wanna come play?"

"Sure." I bought Vince an electric train set for Christmas. Actually Grace and I bought it together, same for Luke's present. She wants to get to know her nephews and she thought that going in with me on a couple of Christmas gifts was a good way to break the ice.

Vince and I play for a few minutes. Luke joins us with his brand new Erector Set, his gift from me and his new aunt.

"I want to meet aunt Grace," Luke says as he sits down with Vince and me. "Can you take me up to see her?"

"As soon as I can Luke, I will," I promise. "I wish I could go up there with you today."

"I asked, Dad said no. I'm sorry."

"Sis," Luke says, whispering in my ear. "Is Grace, is she…like Dad?"

"No, not at all. Your uncle Dr. Bowen isn't either. They're kind, loving people."

"Will you give Aunt Grace this card?" Luke says, handing me an envelope. "Sure," I say. I open the envelope. Inside is a hand drawn card that says "Merry Christmas". Luke penned a short note telling Grace how grateful he was for the Erector Set.

Luke smiles. He can see that I'm impressed by the card and the thought and effort he put into making it.

"How are you doing?" I ask. "Ya know, getting through."

"Luke, I'm sorry that I haven't been around much lately. I love you to death, little brother."

"I love you too, sis. You're dealing with a whole lot. I don't understand it all, but I know you've been busy."

"I'll make it up to you. You'll see."

"Merry Christmas, Sonja," my father says as he walks into the living room. "Merry Christmas, Dad," I respond.

"Nice to see ya. Been a stranger around here for a while now."

"I've been very busy."

"So I hear. How's Walter?"

"I wouldn't know."

"Ya never see him?"

"No, well, rarely. You see him a lot more than me, at church."

"Speakin' of that, when ya comin' back?"

"Coming back? To the church?"

"Yea, we need ya on the piano."

"Never, I'm not coming back."

"Why ya takin' such a hard line on all this?"

"Why don't we sit on the front porch and talk about this Dad."

"Why don't we."

I wasn't expecting to do this before dinner, but "what the heck" I say to myself.

The sooner the better.

We walk out to the porch and sit down. Dad lights a cigarette. "Sonja, Walter loves ya, he really does."

"He may think that he does, whatever, but it doesn't matter. Our marriage is over."

"The Barker's are a fine family, they..."

"I'm not married to the Barker family, I'm married to Walter."

"He's a good man."

"No, he is not a good man. He's a rapist."

"Sonja, ya ought not be sayin' such things. It makes ya sound, well..."

"It makes *me* sound?"

"I promised your mother that I would mind my tongue with you today."

"Dad, we need to get a few things straight between us."

"It's Christmas, Sonja. Maybe we should hold off on …"

"No, it's kinda now or never."

My father is doing what he thinks is his best to behave. He still looks on me as a little girl, not a grown woman—a little girl who should shut up and mind her manners when told to do so.

"Go ahead, say yure peace."

"I forgive you."

"Forgive me for what?"

"For all the cruel and spiteful things that you've done to me and to my brothers and to my mother."

"Now hold on there missy, I may …"

"You're sister really wants to meet you. She asked me if she could call you and wish you Merry Christmas."

"What have I done to ya that was so 'cruel and spiteful'? Ya got a real high opinion of yourself, Sonja. Pride is a dangerous thing."

My attempt to change the subject was obviously a complete failure.

"When you were in the war Dad, what would you have done if someone made fun of one of your buddy's war wounds, saying things like he should just 'get over it' or that his pain was 'no big deal', or something like that?"

"What's that gotta do with what were discussin'?"

"Well, what would you have done?"

"I guess I'd have told the guy to shove it and shut up or I might have just started swingin'."

"So how do you think I felt when you told me that my pain was no big deal, that rape is just something I should 'get over' and ignore?"

"You ain't been in no war. Your husband wants you to do your duty, that's all.

My God in heaven, Sonja."

For the first time, I get it. I truly understand.

Words have no meaning between us because my father hears what he wants to hear and believes what he wants to believe.

What I say does not matter to him, my words count for nothing in his mind. He's just like Walter. They have the same disease.

For my father to tell me I have too much pride...well, that's just flat out amazing. I have forgiven him. I've let it go.

Now I'm letting him go.

"Okay, I've said my peace. Shall we go back inside?"

"Just like that? Ya say those things to me and that's it?"

"Would you like to talk with your sister?"

"Why? I don't know the woman."

"Do you want to know her?"

"Not especially."

"Then let's go back in and have Christmas. We don't need to sit out here any longer."

"What about Walter?"

"What about him?"

"He was hopin' that maybe, it being Christmas and all, that he could stop by and say hello to his wife."

"It's your house but if he comes here, I'm gone. I do not want to talk with him."

"Alright. You're makin' a big mistake, but alright."

I realize as we walk back inside that this is as good as it will ever get between us. My father isn't going to change. I refuse to allow him to make me upset ever again. I will not grant him that kind of power over my emotions any longer.

In my case forgiveness has led to indifference. What an incredible blessing.

CHAPTER FIFTY TWO

Sandy, I love her so much. But she is ditzy. That's her word, "ditzy". She'd forget her head if it wasn't screwed on, to use one of my Grandfather's favorite expressions.

So it's eleven thirty at night, I've thrown on some old pants and a ratty shirt and out the door I go.

What are the odds that Sandy finds her car keys by the time I pick her up? Fifty-fifty. Last time she left them behind the patient files at the nurse's station.

I'm not out much late at night, no reason to be. It's cold, dead of winter. Even in Jacksonville in January it can get cold. I wish I'd brought a sweater.

The hospital is nearly deserted except for a few cars near the front entrance. This isn't the first time that I've been here late at night so nothing is unfamiliar.

As I'm gathering up my purse and locking my doors I see a dark blue Chevy pull up in a hurry. Probably some late night emergency I assume.

I take two steps away from my car and he confronts me. It's Walter.

He and I are standing in the shadows, but bright lights are only a few yards away, the hospital entrance and people maybe twenty yards more.

"Hi, honey."

"Walter," I say, trying my best to sound composed, "what are you doing here?"

"Can't knock on your door now can I."

"What do you want?"

"What do I want…how about to talk with my wife?"

"Walter, I'm in a hurry. I need to go …"

Walter pushes me back against my car door. "You've got time to talk to me."

"How did you know I'd be here?"

"I followed you from where you're staying."

"You were outside my house what, spying on me?"

"Sometimes I sit across the street in the empty house's driveway and watch you come and go. The trees keep you from seeing me."

I'm scared. There are people close by, but not close enough. I know what Walter wants. The same thing he always wants. "Come home Sonja and all will be forgiven."

"Walter, please sign the divorce papers. It's time for you and I to move on."

"I'll never sign those damn papers."

"Walter, please. Try and …"

"You're my wife no matter how confused you are right now."

"I'm not confused. Now, I need to go inside and …"

Walter again pushes me back against the car.

"Some doctor, huh? I figured as much. Out for a little late night roll in the hay?"

"Let me go, Walter. You have no right to keep …"

I feel Walter's hand squeeze against my throat. I can't make a sound.

It's happening again. I let my guard down for just a second and it's happening all over again. Dear God in heaven I…

"Is there a problem here?" a man's voice says.

It's Doctor Carter. He's an OBGYN. He probably got called in to deliver a baby.

Thank you Lord for choosing now for him to leave the hospital. Walter lets me go.

"Yes," I say, rubbing my throat. "This man won't let me go inside to pick up my friend."

"Now honey, please …"

"I'm not your 'honey'. Who the hell are you anyway? I've never met you."

"Alright," Doctor Carter says. "I know who you are young lady. You're Sandy Combs' friend. As for you, sir, I suggest you get back in your car and leave this area.

Otherwise I'm going to call the police and have you arrested for trespassing."

"You're screwing my wife aren't you."

"What did you say?"

I take this moment to move behind Dr. Carter.

"You heard me. She's a married woman. Married to *me*."

Doc takes off his jacket and sets his coat and briefcase on the hood of my car. "You have one second to get the hell out of here or by God sir I will throttle you."

"You don't scare me."

It happened so fast I almost missed it.

Doc kicked Walter in the knee and then spun him around, pinning Walter's arm behind him against his back. Now he has him pressed face first against the hood of my car.

"Like scaring little girls do ya, tough guy?"

"That's assault. Now I'm …"

Doc grabs Walter's head and slams into the car hood.

"If I ever see you around here again I won't call the police. I'll just pull out my gun and handle things myself. Leave this young lady alone. Do you hear me?"

Walter mumbled something, I guess it was yes. Walter is getting a taste of his own medicine.

Few moments in my life have brought me such pleasure.

Doc keeps Walter's arm pinned behind him as he 'escorts' Walter to his car.

I watch as Walter curses Doc from the safety of his locked Chevy and drives away.

"Are you okay? I'm sorry, I don't know your name."

"Sonja Kent. I'm Sandy's roommate."

"You should call the police, Sonja. Let them know this man has bothered you."

"No, Doc. I lied to you. That man is my husband. Soon to be ex-husband, I hope, but we are still legally married."

"Oh," Doc says.

"He has hit me and worse but…what can I do?"

"Indeed," Doc says.

"Thanks," I say, as I turn to walk inside.

"Sonja, be careful. The look in that man's eyes…anyway, watch yourself. Don't go out at night alone for a while."

CHAPTER FIFTY THREE

It was a perfect afternoon in every respect.
In early February in the South sometimes we get these gorgeous days, not too cold, not too hot, just right. The air is pure and crisp. There isn't a cloud in the sky.

We are sitting in Grace's backyard—Grace, Grandma Mary, Sandy and me.

The kids are playing, I'm sipping ice tea, the remains of lunch lay on the table and the Bowen's cocker spaniel is licking my feet.

"Honey, what's going on with Walter? Is he still refusing to grant you a divorce?" Grace asks.

"Yes. I'm frustrated."

"Thomas was no help?"

"No, he only told me what I already knew. If Walter doesn't sign I can ask a judge to make him sign. Even then...well, I'm going to try and get a 'hearing' I think it's called."

"Thomas is a very good lawyer. You can rely on what he says."

"Thanks again for having him speak with me."

"No problem sweetheart, I wish we could do more for you."

"Can I move in? Stay forever?"

"Would you like to?"

"Grace, of course I would…are you kidding?"

"Not at all. Well, maybe not move in but have you considered living in Atlanta or Doraville?"

"Only every time I come up here."

"Sandy and I have been kind of conspiring, hon," Grace admits.

"Oh?"

"I think I have a job up here, starting in April," Sandy says. "Dr. Bowen got me an interview and the chief nurse at the hospital likes me. She has to get it cleared through her department head, but it's pretty much set."

"Oh," I say again, feeling a bit left out.

"Why don't you and Sandy just pull up stakes and move?" Grace asks. "What's keeping you in Jacksonville?"

"What would I do up here? I'm just a dumb kid who never …"

"Ya ain't no 'dumb kid', Sonja," Mary interjects. "Yure about the best piano player around."

"You know band instruments too, from what you told me," Grace adds. "I do, that's true."

"Guess what. Chrysler's Music of Atlanta, they're a big store, is owned by the brother of one of Arthur's oldest friends. Arthur called his pal, one thing led to another and they definitely want to talk with you."

"About a job? In Atlanta?"

"Not exactly. They're expanding to Doraville. They say they'll be ready to open up a store here in two or three months. But they need someone to start right away, to help them set up things, work with their store manager, get all settled in."

"Sure, I mean when…" I'm too excited to speak.

"Call this man tomorrow," Grace says, handing me a business card. "He knows that you live in Jacksonvillle and that you work for the bank, but if he likes you over the phone I'll bet you could set up an interview with him in Atlanta."

I can't believe my luck. Not my luck, my blessings. I'm doing my best not to cry.

Sandy starts asking Grace all sorts of questions about where we might rent a small house or an apartment in Doraville.

I look over at Grandma and my new aunt. They're holding hands.

In just a few short weeks they have become close. It was meant to be. It's beautiful.

Every time I see them together my heart sings. Love, someone told me, is the sweetest music.

Where is my mother? I silently ask myself. She should be here too. "Did Jerry ever call ya back dear?" Grandma asks.

"No, mother. He has no desire to speak with me. What can I do?" Another thing. Grace calls Mary "mother".

"Leave it alone," I caution. "I've learned the hard way with my father that he does what he wants, when he wants, how he wants."

"I'm not giving up," Grace pronounces. "No, you'll probably never give up," I agree.

"Doreen will be overjoyed if you move here, Sonja."

"I think I can help her with the baton."

"I'm sure you can help her in many ways," Grace compliments. Please God, I silently pray, let time stand still. Just for a while. I'm happy, truly happy being right here, right now.

The idea that I might be able to be around music and instruments and musicians every day is almost too good to be true.

As I allow myself to daydream, the first thought that pops into my mind is that I bet I can get a good piano at a great price if I work at a music store.

Sandy and I living together. Her with a great job, me with a great job....

And my music.

What else could I want? What else is there?

CHAPTER FIFTY FOUR

"Could you please explain that to me, one more time?" I ask. I sit up straight in Mr. James' office chair. I need to understand exactly what my lawyer is telling me.

"The Judge said no. He denied our motion to have a hearing on the matter. His response was 'the parties are to pursue reconciliation' for six more months. After that he is open to a re-filing of our petition."

"That's so unfair," I say.

"Mrs. Barker, I could ..."

"Please, call me Sonja or Miss Kent."

"Sonja," Mr. James says, "I'm sorry. Judge Kimball is famous for this, delaying divorce settlements. I'm also fairly certain that he and the Barkers are friendly. I know they both belong to the Yacht Club."

"I need to tell you something else."

"Okay."

"I'm about ninety percent certain that I'm moving to Atlanta next month."

"Really. New job?"

"Yep, it's almost for sure. I have to go up there next weekend for a final interview, but it looks very positive. My aunt and uncle are helping me."

"I'm happy for you but...gosh, I hate to tell you this."

"Go ahead," I say, bracing myself for more bad news.

"If you move out of state Walter will probably be able to delay a divorce almost indefinitely. Since you filed for divorce in Florida and Walter still lives in Florida – do you want the short or long version?"

"Short story will do."

"He can play a lot of games now. Take forever to serve you. Cancel hearings at the last minute. Make you spend more money. Even file motion after motion to dismiss the action and if you fail to show up even once you'll have to start all over again."

"Wonderful," I moan.

"Have you reconsidered my suggestion?"

"I've thought about it, sure."

"And?"

"It would be his word against mine. I know how I come out on that deal."

"This is not the same thing as filing a criminal complaint against him. As I explained you would be ..."

"I get it. We would do it to try and look good in court. I don't think it would change the judge's mind, but it would make me look foolish to my family."

"I don't necessarily disagree, but it is a possible tactic. It might work."

"If you were in my shoes would you do it?"

"Honestly, I couldn't say. I understand your dilemma."

Do you really? I think. You're a nice man Mr. James, but I doubt you "understand my dilemma" because you've never been raped. You've never been threatened by a bully with being raped again.

"How much more money do I owe you?"

"Not a penny more."

"Why? You've done ..."

"Sonja, I want to help you. If we have to go to court again, I'll charge you. Until that time just keep me informed about your circumstances."

Gosh, I think. What a great guy.

Why can't I meet somebody like Mr. James? We shake hands and part ways.

What a way to spend my lunch hour. I'm not looking forward to dinner either.

"Thanks for coming, Sonya," Nelson Barker says. "Yes, we really appreciate it," June adds.

"It's just the three of us, right? I want to be sure …"

"Our son will not be joining us," Nelson assures.

The waiter stops by the table and we place our orders. I order the lobster. I figure that if I have to endure their questioning they can pay for the best meal in the house.

We talk about nothing for a bit and then June declares, "Walter loves you Sonja.

He does not want a divorce."

"What has he told you two about why I want a divorce?"

"He's told us that you two have difficulties in the bedroom." I think, is that really what he told you, Nelson? Who knows.

"Do you folks want the truth or do you want me to lie and sugarcoat it?"

"The truth will do, Sonja," June declares.

"Walter has a serious problem. He believes that he has the right to rape me whenever he chooses."

I stand by for the fireworks. To my surprise none come.

"Walter describes your problems differently, dear,' June says, in between bites of her green salad. "But he told us that you might use the word 'rape'."

"Do you know what happened the night I left him for good?"

"Walter said that you two went to the movies, had a fight in the car and ended up arguing some more when you got home. He left, came to our house and spent the night. The next day when he came home from work you had moved out."

What should I say? I ask myself. I'm tired of being nice. Damn tired.

"Okay. Here is what happened. Walter hit me, knocked me to the ground, stripped off my clothes and drove off, leaving me standing naked by the side of the road. Oh, and he called me a whore. Then he came back a few minutes later and picked me up and drove us home. Once we got there he shoved me down and raped me on the front porch.

Your son is a rapist. He should be arrested and locked up." Now the fireworks come.

"Sonja, keep your voice down. I'm sorry, June. You were right," Nelson says. "You have quite the imagination, Sonja. And quite the foul mouth," June says. I continue to eat my soup and salad.

I'm pretty sure that I won't be here for the main course so I take big bites. "You asked for the truth," I say, wiping my mouth.

"What Walter ever saw in you, I mean to say such …"

"June, I don't want to say 'such things'. You asked for the truth and I told you."

"I think the truth is that you just don't like sex. You don't want children either, that's pretty obvious," Nelson says.

Yep, I was right. No lobster for me. I kinda wanted that lobster too.

"Would you give Walter a message for me?" I ask. The Barkers say nothing as I stand to leave.

"Tell him that he should grow up and sign the divorce papers. Oh, and also tell him that he should think twice about assaulting me in parking lots. People know what really happened between us. People like my lawyer."

I'm calm. Go figure.

I took no pleasure in speaking plainly with my in-laws, but it didn't upset me either.

I am still hungry though.

I wonder, where I can get a cheap lobster meal in Jacksonville?

CHAPTER FIFTY FIVE

"I read every letter, honey. I hope you got mine" Aunt Mabel says. "I did. So much happened while you were gone."

"I hadn't been back to Austria since the war ended. It was well past time to pay my respects."

Aunt Mabel was home now, thank you Jesus. While she was traveling we kept in contact through letters, but I am not the best letter writer in the world. If I manage to scratch out a couple of pages every two weeks I'm doing real well.

Mabel came straight here from the airport in Miami. Sandy's mother was kind enough to drive her to Jacksonville. When the weekend comes I'm taking her to meet her new sister-in-law Grace in Doraville and then home to Augusta.

Mabel is all settled in to my room and the three of us are drinking tea on the back screened porch.

"Leaving Walter was the right thing to do," Mabel offers.

"I kinda had no choice unless I wanted to be raped over and over again. That gets tiresome."

"Be careful who you use that language with, Sonja. People take offense at such terms."

"Are you one of those people?" I ask.

"For heaven's sakes no. Walter deserves, well, I'll restrain my tongue."

"No need to, not around here," Sandy says, grinning.

"Walter needs a good ass whipping," Mabel declares. "If Porter were still alive he would have given him one too, I assure you."

"Be nice if I had a father like Porter."

"I'm going to speak with Jerry tomorrow. I still can't believe that he didn't come to your defense."

"Nah, no one did."

"What am I, no one?" Sandy whines.

"You're my bestest, ditzy, carrot top girlfriend. And you certainly did come to my defense."

"Thank you. I guess you do have some brains after all." We both giggle. Mabel clearly loves our banter.

"You girls are going to absolutely love Atlanta. I could not be happier for you both and I'll only be a couple of hours away."

"Well, I guess I should tell you guys. I may not be moving to Atlanta."

"Sonja!" Sandy shrieks. "That can't be true."

"Yesterday Mr. James told me that if I move Walter can put off the divorce for a long time. If I stay I might be able to speed it up some, but there are no guarantees. I have to be free of him."

"Oh Sonja, don't let Walter do that to you," Mabel says. "What she said," Sandy echoes.

"I'm just not sure anymore. What if he tries to hang on forever? What if I never get divorced?"

"Honey, I'm no expert on legal matters but I've lived a long life. Things like this…sooner or later they resolve themselves. Walter will get tired of playing games. Maybe he will find someone new. He will want a divorce then for sure."

"It's a nightmare, Aunt Mabel. Why didn't I see this coming? I was foolish to marry Walter."

"You are a young girl. Young girls make mistakes, that's part of being a young girl."

"He seemed nice enough to you though didn't he?"

"Husbands are like cars. You can find one that looks good, sounds right and has a nice ride. But you never know whether or not you bought a lemon 'til you drive it for a while."

"Ain't that the truth," Sandy concurs.

"You married your father, Sonja," Mabel says, in a matter of fact manner.

I'm taken aback. Of course Mabel is exactly right, but to hear someone else say aloud what I've secretly accused myself of doing for so long is shocking.

"You're…you're right," I admit. "I was a damn fool."

"Don't go beating yourself up too much, angel. Men like your father and Walter; you just aren't old enough yet to know how to deal with them."

I have to ask. I've wanted to know the answer to this question since I was a little girl. "What is it between you and my father? When you say jump, he says how high. No one else can …"

"Jerry has a thing for me, hon. Always has, since Porter brought me back from Austria."

"My father is… he's…" The words won't come.

"Jerry never asked me to sleep with him or anything, but over the years he's made it plain that he, well, he desires me. That's the simplest way to put it."

"Does my mother know about his 'desire'?"

"We've never discussed the subject, but Faye isn't blind, or stupid. I'm sure she knows. But so what? It doesn't mean much, except to Jerry."

"I'm not following you."

"To Jerry I'll always be forbidden fruit; the beautiful girl from far away with the nice curves and the strange accent. I would never let him touch me, Lord no, but I flirt with him just enough to let him think that maybe someday, someway, he might have a chance."

"You play with him like that?"

"Oh yes, for ten years plus now, angel. It gives me some leverage with him and, to be honest, I enjoy the game. Porter thought it was the funniest thing in the world."

"Uncle Porter knew?"

"Of course! That's what made it fun. Brothers are always competing. Believe me; Porter knew that the last person in the world I would ever consider sleeping with was your father."

"I'm so naïve."

"You do need to grow up a bit when it comes to men, Sonja dear. Men and women play games. You're way too straightforward. Try and be a little more clever and you'll soon see that men will become much easier to deal with."

"You're right, I guess." While I wasn't sold on her methods, I certainly could not argue with Mabel's results.

"Go to Atlanta, Sonja. There is nothing for you here but bad memories."

"I want to go, Aunt Mabel, so bad. I'm just not sure it's the right thing to do."

"Are there more reasons than just the divorce?"

"Luke and Vince. They need me too. So does my mother."

"Faye made you feel guilty for leaving, did she?"

"Not intentionally."

Mabel laughs. "Oh, it was intentional honey. Believe that."

"Luke and Vince are still youngsters and my father, you know, he's a tyrant. They need me around a whole lot more than I've been lately. Now that I'm single again I can …"

"Sonja," Mabel says as she reaches over and squeezes my hand. "Think of your life as a keyboard; 'Sonja Kent's Keyboard'. The keys will only make beautiful music if you play them in the proper order, with finesse, with skill, with love. The Good Lord has set the symphony of your life before you. Play the music. Don't let anything or anyone stand in your way."

What a lovely sentiment, I thought.

Miss Bloom often reminded me that every day is a gift and we have no right to waste even a moment. We are renters of our bodies, not owners, according to her. She believes that someday the Owner is going to ask us to account for our blessings.

What would I say to Jesus if I don't go to Atlanta? That I was too afraid to go?

That I didn't trust Him to look after me and my brothers? "Have I told you how much I love you?" I say.

"Thanks, sugar. I love you too," Sandy replies as she bats her eyes at me, lightening the moment with humor.

"Where did you find this girl?" Mabel teases. "We sort of found each other," Sandy replies. "She's a keeper," I say, beaming at my best friend. "So you're going?" Sandy asks.

"Yes, I'm going. Someone has to feed you. What would happen if you lost your keys or your purse in Atlanta? You need looking after."

We laugh some more.

We spend the rest of the day laughing, chatting and planning. I am so blessed. Despite it all, so very blessed.

CHAPTER FIFTY SIX

"Thank you, Mr. Larsen. It's so nice of you ..."
I stand up, take a couple of steps and give Mr. Larsen a hug and a kiss on the cheek.

"Sonja, my gosh..." His face turns red from embarrassment. "Would you like a hug and a kiss too Mr. Peterson?" I tease. "Love one, but the missus might object, ya know."

We smile and chuckle.

I'll miss these guys. Both of them are good men who did their best to help me.

They are great bankers too, very professional. God bless them.

For Mr. Larsen to give me a two hundred dollar bonus...well, I can't say I deserve it, but I'll take it. I need every nickel right now.

"So tell us all about your new life," Mr. Larsen says.

We are having my farewell lunch at Reggie's, a very nice cafe on Main Street.

Today is my last day. I leave for Atlanta on Monday.

"Well, for the first couple of months I'll be helping Mr. Wells, that's the store manager, put together the new store. I need to set up the shelves, the stockroom and interview the clerk candidates. He also wants me to visit the junior and senior high schools in the area and any other groups that regularly buy musical instruments. Another part of my job is to become friendly with local bands, you know, get the store's name out there."

"Mr. Wells is the store manager?"

"Yes."

"What's your title?"

"Assistant Manager, can you believe that? Me, an Assistant Manager!"

The idea of being an assistant manager of anything was still new and exciting. "You will do well, Sonja," Mr. Larsen says.

"I agree. You know, if you'd have stayed we had plans for you, Sonja."

"Really, Mr. Peterson?"

"First as a teller, but then...well, we lost one. But we're both pleased that you are moving on with your life, but you will be missed."

He approached without me spotting him.

"Hello honey," Walter says as he stands beside me at the table. Mr. Larsen gives Walter a wary stare.

"Walter, I...hello," I say. The last thing I want or need is a scene with Walter in front of my now ex-bosses.

"I don't believe that I've met these gentlemen."

I introduce Walter. Then I say, "Is there something I can ..."

"No, honey. I was walking by and saw you having lunch and wanted to share the good news with you, that's all."

My heart leaps.

Is it possible? Has he finally signed the divorce papers? "I got the job."

"The job?"

"Yes, the one we talked about. I'm going to work at Coca Cola part time and I start my classes at Georgia Tech this summer. I'm moving to Atlanta. In fact, I've been hunting for a place in Doraville so we can stay close and continue to work on our marriage."

I'm stunned, truly in a state of shock.

From the look on my face Mr. Larsen can tell that this is the first I've heard of any of this.

He has to be kidding, I tell myself.

There is no way Walter would leave Barker's Sporting Goods. The business is his; maybe sooner rather than later if Nelson retires early.

"Is this a joke, Walter?" I somehow manage to eke out. I'm shaking all over and the tears are about to flow. I simply cannot hide my emotions. "No, of course not, dear," Walter says.

He is putting on a show for Mr. Peterson and Mr. Larsen—Walter at his most charming self.

"Mr. Barker," Mr. Larsen says, "I don't mean to intrude on your personal business, but Sonja has been very open with us about the state of her relationship with you. With all due respect, you have upset her with this news. Perhaps you could discuss this with her at another time."

Thank you Mr. Larsen, I shout in my mind.

"Perhaps you, sir, should consider who you go smooching with in public. She may be your girlfriend, but Sonja is my wife."

Mr. Larsen is a slightly built man, almost delicate. I don't think anyone would consider him to be a physical threat.

Regardless, Mr. Larsen is offended, greatly offended, by Walter's accusation. I can see it in his eyes. His face is turning red again, and not from embarrassment.

"Mr. Barker, you have no right to insult me or my integrity. I have been married for over ..."

"You just kissed my wife. Right here in public. That gives me the right to ..."

"Stop it, Walter," I say.

For some reason I am suddenly completely composed. Aunt Mabel's advice about being more 'clever' with men immediately comes to mind.

"Sonja, we need to ..."

"You need to leave, right now. See that waiter over there?" I say, pointing at my friend Ben, a two hundred and fifty pound former Andrew Jackson football player who I knew from school and always says hello to me at the bank. He's had a crush on me forever.

Ben has been paying attention. He can see that something is developing at the table. He points at himself asking me if I need his help. I hold up my palm, signaling not yet.

"So what?" Walter says.

"That's my boyfriend. If you have a problem with me, take it up with him." I stand up and signal to Ben that I need his help.

Walter says, "I knew it. I knew you were seeing someone."

"Yea, you're a genius Walter. I think it's time that you and Ben had a conversation."

Ben is a few feet away now and he is taking off his smock. Walter turns and walks away.

"Sonja?" Ben says. "You need some help?"

"No, hon," I say, giving my big friend are very affectionate hug. "I just wanted to say good-bye. I'm moving to Atlanta."

I had intended to say goodbye to Ben after lunch anyway.

As I look up I see Walter standing outside on the sidewalk watching us.

After I introduce Ben to Mr. Larsen and Mr. Peterson I say, "Can I have a kiss goodbye?"

"Sure," Ben says, not believing his luck. I lay one on him; a good, long deep kiss.

Looking up I make sure that I make eye contact with Walter. When I do, he storms off.

Walter is moving to Atlanta?

Please God, tell me this is just a bad dream.

CHAPTER FIFTY SEVEN

"C'mon, hon. There are only a few more loads to go," Sandy encourages. "Okay, sorry. I'll try and keep up," I say.

"You still want to go to church right?" Sandy asks. "Yes, of course."

"Have you eaten anything today?"

"No," I answer.

"All this work and no food...I'm feeding you? Now I know you're in trouble."

"Walter is moving to Atlanta. I still can't ..."

"We can talk about it some more Sonja, if you want," Sandy says, "but I still say it's a bunch of bull."

"I knew that he would find out sooner or later that I was moving, I was expecting that, but I ..."

"It's bull. He just said that to make you angry, get you upset."

"It worked."

"Did you ever tell Ben that you told Walter he was your boyfriend?"

"No. I thought about it, but decided against that move. Ben might get the wrong idea and then. oh hell. I'm so tired of all this nonsense."

"Ben is a really good looking guy. Maybe…"

"Sandy."

"Sorry, stay on point. I know. No horsing around."

"I wish I felt like horsing around."

"Do you feel like picking up some more boxes? The truck is nearly full."

"Okay, okay."

We finish loading the Scott's old Ford truck with our stuff. All we have to do tomorrow is drive away.

I was really, really looking forward to tomorrow.

It was to be my liberation day, the day I started my new life.

Now it seems that I might just be dragging my old life to a new place. I'm thankful that it's time for church.

Prayer is what I need right now and lots of it.

I'll miss Sandy's congregation.

Grace and Arthur are Presbyterians too so I'm fairly certain that I'll become one officially sooner or later.

I'm comfortable here, more comfortable than I was with the Baptists. Maybe that's because I chose this church, it wasn't chosen for me.

But anywhere Jesus is praised I feel at home. As the Scriptures say, God does not live in buildings; He lives in each of us.

Before the service begins I close my eyes and pray. God, I silently ask, I need your help.

I need You to help me to forgive Walter.

I'm having terrible thoughts about him, wishing him ill.

I don't want to be that kind of person. I know that is not the kind of person You want me to be.

So, God, if Walter is really following me to Atlanta show me what to do. I ask that you set me free of him, Lord.

But not my will, Your will be done.

Is asking You for a divorce a sin? I don't think it is in my case, but You have to tell me, Lord. Let me be led and not try to lead.

God bless Walter. God bless my father.

God bless my brothers and my mom.

And God bless Sandy.

Oh, and I almost forgot. God bless Ralphie too. I'm getting attached to that dog. I feel better after I pray. I always do.

After the service Sandy and I say goodbye to everyone. While I haven't known these people for very long, I like them.

Sandy I decide to go to Ozzies for a burger and fries and then take one last, long walk on the beach.

We don't make it back home until nearly eight o'clock.

Nelson Barker is sitting in his car waiting for us in front of our house when we arrive.

As Sandy and I pull in Nelson gets out of his car. This first thing I do is look around and make sure that he is alone.

Seeing that no one else is with him I breathe a sigh of relief.

"Nelson?" I say, walking from our car port to greet him as walks up the driveway. "Can I help you?"

"Sonja, let's go inside."

Nelson is very upset. His eyes are bloodshot. His shirt is untucked and his pants are wrinkled. I have never seen Nelson Barker in public unkempt. He simply does not go out if he doesn't look his best.

A million thoughts are racing through my head as we go in and sit down around our small kitchen table. Obviously Nelson is here about Walter. What has he done now? "Sonja, I tried to reach you earlier. I think I just missed you at the Presbyterian church. I don't want to you to think I didn't try..."

Nelson starts to cry. Nelson Barker crying? Another first. I'm no longer concerned, I'm petrified.

What has Walter done?

"Nelson, my heavens. Sandy, could you get him a drink or something?" Sandy is scared to death too. She pours Nelson a glass of water.

He gulps it down like he hasn't had drink for days. "Nelson, what's wrong?" I ask.

"Walter is dead."

"What?" I say, not believing my ears.

"Late last night he was driving along the coast road. The police say that there was an open bottle of whiskey, almost empty, in his car. He swerved and ran into a big rig truck, head on. He was killed instantly."

Nelson is really balling now. I look at Sandy, begging her with my eyes for guidance. What do I say? What do I do?

The thought, "comfort the man" bursts to the front of my mind.

I stand up and hug Nelson. He stands and hugs me back, very hard. There is one thing I just cannot do though.

I wish I could. I feel like a terrible person for not doing it. I simply cannot cry.

"Nelson," I say, as I let him go. "Walter drinks on occasion, but he hates whiskey. Are you sure that part of the story is accurate?"

"The police don't make those things up, Sonja." No, I think, I'm sure they don't.

"Nelson, I'm...sorry." My sentiments don't sound genuine at all.

"Walter loved you, Sonja. He was very upset when we saw him earlier on Saturday at the church. He said that you told him you had a boyfriend and that ..."

"Nelson, please. First of all I don't have a boyfriend. But even if I did..." I regretted the words as they were coming out of my mouth.

"Why couldn't you just love my son?" Walter says, as he begins another crying episode.

Lord in heaven, I pray. I do not know what to say or do. I'm paralyzed.

Sandy looks at me and tells me with her eyes that she would rather be anywhere in the world other than right here, right now.

But I need her and she knows it so she doesn't leave.

"Nelson," I somehow manage to say, "I meant it when I said that I was sorry for your loss. I sincerely am."

"You hated Walter. I wish I knew why....I just don't understand. June is absolutely beside herself."

Sometimes the Holy Spirit just takes over.

I've been in that circumstance a few times in my life. No one without faith would ever understand it.

When it happens your words are not your own. Your will is completely subjected to His will.

At this very moment I know that no good, by good I mean pleasing to God, can come from me being anything but empathetic to this man and his family. It is not my place to seek vengeance or to prove a point or to do anything other show Christian mercy to a soul in need.

"Nelson, your son loved you. He told me often how much he respected you as a man and as a father. He loved his mother too. May the peace of Christ be with you both."

Now I can cry.

My tears are not for Walter, but for his family, for those that loved him. While I no longer love him, for a brief moment I did.

I am reminded that all of us, me and everyone else, are struggling sinners.

While none of that changes the pain I endured at his hand, Walter is answering to the Lord for his sins, just as someday I will have to answer for mine.

I forgive you Walter, I silently pray. I truly forgive you.

Nelson and I sit up until midnight talking. Poor Sandy was able to make a graceful exit around nine thirty.

I do not share anything with him but good memories about Walter. I do a whole lot more listening than talking.

When Nelson leaves it's just me and Ralphie in the kitchen.

There aren't any dishes to put away or chores to do because this house will empty in a few hours.

I give Ralphie a late night snack from the bottom of an old dog food bag and make a cup of tea in an old cup we're leaving behind.

The silence roars—my life is no longer the same. Walter is dead.

My God.

CHAPTER FIFTY EIGHT

I love our little home. It's filled with friendship, laughter and peace.

Sandy will be back any minute and then I'll be leaving. But right now I'm enjoying a cup of tea in the quiet twilight and petting my dog.

We took Ralphie with us to Doraville. Bart Scott said, in a joking manner, that we had "ruined" his dog. Ralphie became very attached to Sandy and me from the moment we came to live in the Scott's guest house.

Some things, I suppose, are simply meant to be.

But figuring out those things that are meant to be and separating them from those we think, or believe or want to believe are meant to be, that's the challenge.

That's what's called wisdom. I take another sip of tea.

It's been almost two months since Walter's death. Grace helped me through the tasks involved in wrapping up Walter's affairs. Since we were not legally divorced, I was responsible for seeing to it that all the loose ends were tied up.

One of those loose ends was a five thousand dollar life insurance policy payable to me.

As I sit here in my kitchen on a Friday evening considering all that's happened I stare at the insurance check and wonder, what will I do with five thousand dollars?

The only thing I know for sure is that I am buying a piano for our front room.

Chrysler's Store will make me a great deal on a used Baldwin.

Sandy and I discussed it and she would love for me to play for her; she says it would not be an intrusion; it would be a blessing, to have our home filled with music.

I'm going to save the rest of the money. If I have a piano I don't need much else.

One of my brothers might need help, or perhaps my mom. You never know.

I am going to make regular trips to Jacksonville to see my brothers. I am so glad that Luke will be spending the entire month of July with Grace and me, splitting time between our houses. Luke has cousins that he really wants and needs to get to know.

I take another sip.

For the Memorial Day weekend we're driving down to Grandma and Grandpa's house. Arthur and Grace love the property. They love it so much they are going to buy it and let my grandparents live there until they both pass on. Arthur says that eventually Augusta will grow and the farm will not be isolated anymore, it will be a suburb. Then, he says, the land will become quite valuable.

I finish my tea, walk to the sink and wash the cup. I look outside. The last rays of light are peeking over the horizon. The sky is a beautiful light orange color.

I think about Walter. I take a second to silently pray for his soul. I'm not a girl anymore, I'm all grown up.

I've learned the hard way that my life is my responsibility. I have to live with the consequences of my choices.

I know that Nelson and June Barker, and probably most of the congregation of the First Baptist Church, think I am to blame for Walter's demise.

That is something I cannot change.

I recall the first time Walter and I ever spent a few moments alone together outside of the church.

Pastor Walker asked us to visit a family whose son had committed suicide over the pain he felt when his fiancé broke up with him.

The fiancé, that poor girl...what was her name? Julie Reed.

Julie was saddled with the blame for a young boy's death because she chose not to be his wife. People quickly and callously jumped to that conclusion because that was the easy way out.

More wisdom—it is very unfair to judge people from afar or make assumptions without knowing all the facts. It's tough enough to judge even when you are directly involved and know all the facts.

Julie and I will always have something in common – certain people will use us as scapegoats to make them feel better about the death of a loved one.

As for me, all I can do is give it all to my Merciful Savior. He is alone is our judge.

I hear Sandy coming in the front door. She's calling out my name. We're headed to Atlanta to visit one of Sandy's friends.

It's time to go. "Coming!" I yell.

I put away the dishcloth and turn off the kitchen light. As I grab my purse I consider a final thought before I go.

Life goes on – through the pain, the trials and the joy, life goes on.

All I can do is play the sweetest music I can and trust in God to take care of the rest.

www.ingramcontent.com/pod-product-compliance
Lightning Source LLC
LaVergne TN
LVHW011933070526
838202LV00054B/4611